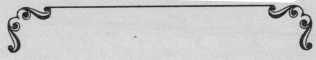

"Look at me," he demanded, but she refused. He held her easily with one hand and brought his other up beneath her chin, forcing her head up. One teardrop rolled forlornly down her cheek.

"Do not cry, little one." With gentle fingers, he brushed the tears from her cheek and then traced the outline of her lips. He looked at her long lashes, now wet with tears, and knew an urge to kiss them. Instinctively, he released her arm, and slid his hand around her back, drawing her closer.

She stared up at him, unable to move. His eyes seemed to probe the depths of her soul. She knew he was going to kiss her, and she was powerless to stop him. Worse, she did not wish to. She felt his warm breath against her cheek, and parted her lips slightly. She lifted her head a fraction of an inch, and half closed her eyes. . . .

Also by Jeanne Carmichael
Published by Fawcett Books:

LADY SCOUNDREL*

*Forthcoming

LORD OF THE MANOR

Jeanne Carmichael

FAWCETT CREST • NEW YORK

A Fawcett Crest Book
Published by Ballantine Books
Copyright © 1994 by Carol Quinto

All rights reserved under International and Pan-American Copyright Conventions. Published in the United States of America by Ballantine Books, a division of Random House, Inc., New York, and simultaneously in Canada by Random House of Canada Limited, Toronto.

Library of Congress Catalog Card Number: 94-94398

ISBN 0-449-22315-9

Manufactured in the United States of America

First Edition: December 1994

10 9 8 7 6 5 4 3 2 1

For cherished friend and valued mentor,
JAYNE ROSS
with love and gratitude
for her encouragement and belief in me.

Chapter 1

Miss Althea Underwood usually enjoyed reading in the peaceful ambience of the blue drawing room. It was smaller than most of the rooms at Keswick Manor and caught the afternoon sunlight. Several years previously Althea had relegated its heavy, dark furniture and dismal dark blue curtains to the attics. She'd re-covered the remaining sofas and chairs with a light floral pattern. The color of the roses in the sofa was picked up by the same soft shade in the new curtains. Although the room was still referred to as the blue drawing room, rose was now the predominant color, and the room was particularly Althea's own.

The French doors were set open to catch whatever breeze there might be, and the tantalizing aroma of freshly cut grass drifted in, distracting Althea from her novel. She laid aside the book, her gaze drawn to the sweeping green lawns beyond the terrace. The contrast of the sunlit expanses against the darker, shaded areas beneath the trees was an inviting one. She contemplated a stroll in the gardens after tea, but Mrs. Pennington had already brought in the tray and Althea knew that

Meredith and Aunt Pysie would join her within a few minutes.

She heard the door open and glanced around with a smile. Dismay abruptly altered her features and she uttered a small gasp of amazement. "Keswick!"

The man remained in the doorway, observing her astonishment with a cool, superior sort of smile.

Althea could scarcely credit her eyes and sat, momentarily stunned. Andrew Carlyle, the Earl of Keswick, was the last man in the world she expected to see—the last man she wanted to see. She gripped the arms of her chair as though it would keep her world from crumbling.

Keswick did nothing to ease her discomfort. He stood at ease, a trace of arrogance in the proud tilt of his head.

Althea stared numbly. Every inch of his towering height, from the clothes he wore with casual elegance to the tips of his Hessian boots, proclaimed the man the lord of the manor. His dark eyes swept over her with seeming indifference. Then, as if finding little of interest there, his gaze traveled around the room. He did not even grant her the courtesy of looking at her when he spoke but crossed instead to the French doors.

"Cheever told me I'd find you in here, Miss Underwood. You have changed very little, but I hardly recognize the blue room and would not know it at all, save for the view."

She stood hastily, a deep blush betraying her agitation. In the space of a moment he had managed to put her in the wrong, and she struggled for composure. "I am sorry if you dislike the changes, my lord, but your aunt and I agreed the room was too dark as it was."

"Still leaping to conclusions, Althea? I did not say I disliked the room, merely that I did not recognize it. But it is of no moment." He drew off his gloves and carelessly tossed them on the table. "I see I have arrived in time for tea." His brows lifted in mock astonishment as he surveyed the elaborate array of cakes and sandwiches. "Are you, perhaps, expecting guests?"

"No, my lord. That is, your aunt and Meredith will be down in a moment, but no one outside the family. I . . . I engaged a new chef some years ago, and he believes in a substantial tea." Mindful that it was the earl who footed the bill for such expenses, she added, "I can assure you it does not go to waste."

"Calm yourself, my dear. I have no quarrel with you over *that*. Indeed, it appears an improvement, if I correctly recall the meals once served in this house."

Belatedly, Althea realized that Keswick could not be seated while she stood. Resuming her place, she gestured to the chair opposite and endeavored to regain some measure of poise. She poured him a cup of tea, trying to remain composed under the heat of his gaze. Vainly, she wished she had not chosen today to wear an old muslin dress that was sadly out of style.

Keswick lounged in the chair opposite, his long legs stretched out before him. His heavy boots, for all their exquisite style and shine, looked out of place against the delicate pattern of the rug. Indeed the man himself overpowered the small room.

3

He, however, did not appear ill at ease and leisurely studied Althea, deciding she had only improved with age. Her dark brown hair, which had once been rigorously tortured into the latest style, was brushed back from her face and fell in soft curls to her shoulders. The effect enhanced the perfect oval of her face, and her large brown eyes and high cheekbones appeared more pronounced. The style gave her a softer, more feminine look, but Keswick did not doubt that Althea still had a temper to be reckoned with and wondered how soon it would be before she ripped up at him. He had not long to wait.

Althea, unsettled by his bold regard, passed him the cup of tea. The saucer trembled in her fingers and Keswick steadied her hand. She drew back at once, irritated that he still had the power to discompose her. Her expressive eyes mirrored her resentment, though she kept her voice deceptively mild. "You might have sent us some word of your arrival, my lord."

"To what purpose, my dear? Keswick Manor is still *my* home, after all."

"One would not know it, sir, after an absence of five years," she retorted, her eyes dangerously bright. "Had I but known you intended to pay us a call, I would have made arrangements to visit elsewhere."

"Indeed?" He smiled, but it was not a smile calculated to soothe. "You may still do so, if you wish, but I fear your visit will have to be of some duration. I am home for good."

"Surely you jest?" She cast about desperately for some means of discouraging him. "What possible

4

attraction could Keswick Manor hold for you? We live quietly here, my lord."

"Perhaps my tastes have changed, and it is quiet I desire," he said. His eyes mocked her, dared her to gainsay him. Then he added in the unrelenting tone she remembered too well, "And there is my daughter."

"Meredith? Why, you did not even wish to see her when she was born! The child has no notion who you are."

"Precisely, and that is a situation which it is time I remedied. However, do not feel that you must remain if my presence here offends you."

She drew in a sharp breath and lifted her head, meeting his gaze squarely. "Do not mistake me for my cousin, sir. Deborah may have been intimidated by your tactics, but I am not. Nothing would induce me to leave Meredith alone with a man of your repute."

Keswick stared at her for a moment, the silence stretching uncomfortably between them, but she would not back down. She straightened her shoulders and fiercely met his gaze. His face was unreadable. Then Althea fancied she caught a brief flash of annoyance in his dark eyes, precisely the sort of look one would bestow on a pesky fly.

When he finally spoke, it was in a languid drawl that held no trace of anger. "You must do as you please, of course. I assure you I have no desire to part you from the child."

"How very *kind* of you," she retorted, and rose. Her brown eyes flashed with sparks of anger. "I suppose it is too much to expect you to honor your wife's last wish? Deborah requested that I take sole charge of Meredith."

5

"Now why does that not surprise me? Naturally, Deborah would feel such a great beast as myself could not be trusted with a child. I expected nothing less of her, but is that your judgment as well?" he asked, a trace of bitterness underlying his words. When she did not reply immediately, he laughed dryly. "Come, my dear, you must own your cousin was a spoiled, vapid creature with not two thoughts in her head and an overworked imagination."

"She was a gentle, sensitive young girl. And if you had handled her properly, she would have worshipped you. Instead, you terrified her."

"Terrified her?" He stood, too, and towered over her.

For an instant she feared she'd gone beyond the line. Then Keswick turned away, disgust on his handsome features.

"Deborah would have been frightened of a rabbit. She was lost without her mama to direct her every move. Afraid to speak to the chef, afraid to direct Mrs. Pennington, afraid of her own shadow. Need I remind you, I left her when she was breeding not because I wanted to get away but because it was what Deborah preferred?"

There was some truth in his words, but Althea would not admit it. She still blamed him for Deborah's death, and his sudden appearance revived the old sorrow. The doctor had said her poor cousin did not have the will to live. Even the knowledge that she'd given birth to a little girl had failed to revive her. Althea took a few steps away from Keswick, moving toward the open French doors.

"Uncle John should never have agreed to your

marriage. I hold him as much to blame as I do you, but at least he cared for Deborah, and in the eyes of the world it was an excellent match. But you—why could you not have wed Lady Edgemere? The *on-dit* was—" She broke off abruptly. The rumors concerning Lady Edgemere were not the sort an unmarried woman of five-and-twenty should know. Althea could not look at him, but she heard the derisive amusement in his voice.

"I believe you have answered your own question, my dear. The Countess of Keswick must be above reproach."

"But not the earl?" She couldn't resist taunting him, and turned.

"It is the way of the world," he said with a shrug of his broad shoulders. "I did not make the rules. As for choosing Deborah, she was not my choice. My aunts and your uncle arranged the marriage between them, as you must know. I agreed because it was time I married and produced an heir."

"And you did not care a whit about Deborah. You took a shy, sensitive girl to wife and never even tried to—"

"Careful, my dear girl. I realize you were as close as sisters, but there are things you do not know, Althea, and which I do not intend to discuss with you, not now, not ever. What passed in private between my wife and me is none of your affair. If you wish to remain here, concern yourself with Meredith all you wish, but I give you fair warning: Do not step beyond that line."

His voice was hard, and the deadly look in his eyes sent a chill through her. Involuntarily, she looked away but dared to defy him a little. "You still have not an heir, my lord."

7

"That, my dear Althea, is the other reason I have come home. I turn five-and-thirty next month, and as I am unwilling to see George Selwyn step into my shoes, I must look around for a wife."

"You approve not of your cousin, my lord?" she inquired sweetly.

Keswick eyed her warily. She appeared the picture of innocence, but her smile made him uneasy. Watching her carefully, he answered, "I've nothing against Selwyn, but we have always disagreed on most matters. And he is not, after all, a Carlyle."

"Some might consider that a boon," she countered, eyes downcast. She anticipated a quick retort, and his silence unnerved her. She looked up to see him studying her, his eyes narrowed and thoughtful.

The door opened before he could speak. A short, rotund lady whirled into the room and threw herself into Keswick's arms, chattering all the while. "Well, upon my soul. I could not believe my ears when Mrs. Pennington told me you were home, Andrew. Not that I mean to say I disbelieved her, because I am quite certain she is the soul of honesty and would never utter an untruth, but we were never expecting you. At least I do not believe we were?"

Keswick laughed aloud as he disengaged her plump arms and led her to a chair by the tea tray. "Aunt Pysie, it is delightful to see you again. I vow you have not changed a bit."

"Gammon, Andrew. Why, anyone with eyes in his head can see I have gained a few pounds, though I do try to diet. It is dreadfully hard, how-

8

ever, since we got the new chef," she said, her eyes drawn to the tea tray. "Do sit down, Andrew, for you have grown so tall I must strain my neck to look up at you. Have you tried any of these cakes yet?"

She passed him a plate, her eyes fondly taking in every detail of his appearance, and confided, "You look wonderfully well, Andrew. Indeed, much better than I expected, after hearing all those terrible rumors about you. I quite thought you would have grown rather stout and possess a red nose like your uncle Albert." She turned and added for Althea's benefit, "Poor dear Albert died of excessive drink, you know."

Althea nodded soberly, but her eyes were brimming with laughter and she did not dare look at Keswick.

Aunt Pysie took no notice. "You are just as handsome as ever, Andrew, and my gracious, not even a gray hair to your head. There can be no justice in the world, but I expect it is the Carlyle legacy. Your papa's hair was still quite black when he died. Mine comes from my mother, alas, as you can see from all the gray. Why, I have to resort to wearing a wig when we are formal, which is not very often, because we live quietly here, and entertain but rarely. Still, we shall have to give a dinner now that you are back. How long do you mean to stay?"

"I am home for good, Aunt," he replied, but his attention was riveted on the child who hesitated just inside the door. She was a tiny, slender girl with riotous black curls and large dark eyes. His daughter. Just saying the words to himself gave him an odd sort of feeling.

His aunt, observing the bemused look in his eyes, glanced around and beckoned to the child. "Meredith, come in, my dear. We have a wonderful surprise for you. Your papa is home."

Five-year-old Meredith was not a shy child, for she was used to conversing with Aunt Pysie, her adopted aunt Althea, and Miss Appletree. She advanced slowly, but only to give herself time to observe the man before her. She finally stood directly in front of Keswick and, with hands clasped behind her, stared up into eyes just a shade darker than her own.

Althea, seated across from him, wondered what Meredith saw there, for without warning the child suddenly cast herself into his arms and warmly kissed his cheek.

Keswick held her gently. She had his hair and eye coloring, but her body felt incredibly fragile and slender. He feared he might crush her without ever realizing it.

Meredith had no such fears and entwined her arms tightly about his neck.

Aunt Pysie dabbed at her eyes. "How very touching. Why, she has never laid eyes on you, but it is almost as though she knew you, Andrew. Meredith rarely goes to strangers so easily—she has the Carlyle reserve. But then I suppose you are not really a stranger, are you? I mean, you are her papa."

Althea was not as moved by the reunion. "Get down now, Meredith, you are crushing your . . . your papa's coat."

"It does not matter," Keswick said with a smile for his daughter, and bent his dark head close to the child's. "I want to hear all about you,

Meredith. What you do all day, what you like and what you dislike. Tell me, little one, do you ride?"

"Yes, Papa. I have my own pony, and I ride every morning with Aunt Thea. I have excellent bottom."

Keswick hid a smile and looked at Althea. "Might I be permitted to join you tomorrow?"

"Why, you must do just as you please, my lord. As you pointed out, Keswick Manor is *your* home, and I would certainly not presume to dictate to you."

"Then you have changed a great deal," he said.

"Oh, dear me," Aunt Pysie muttered. "Althea, dearest, I am certain Andrew does not mean to . . . That is . . . Andrew, you must realize Althea has managed the house for several years now, and wonderfully, too, I might add. Why, the chef you had here was a disgrace to his name, and I am positive he imbibed quite frequently, for there can be no other excuse for the terrible meals he set before us. Why, you would not credit that once he served us a capon that was raw—indeed, it was, Andrew—but that is another tale," she said, pausing for breath.

Keswick, his head bent close to his daughter's, paid no attention. Althea picked up her needlepoint and busily plied her needle while the tension in the room thickened. Aunt Pysie redoubled her efforts.

"What I mean to say is, your servants were quite slothful, Andrew, and we were vastly uncomfortable until Althea took matters in hand. Now the house runs remarkably well and I know you will not wish to overset our arrangements. Of course I

11

understand some things must change, now that you are home, but I would not for the world have you upset Althea. . . ."

"I plan no immediate changes, Aunt," Keswick soothed, mindful of his daughter's wide eyes. "And I have no doubt that Althea is more capable of running the house than I could ever be. The servants will continue to receive their orders from her."

"There, I knew there was no need to worry. I always believed you a reasonable man even if the rumors that reached us were, that is to say, we heard reports that—well, no doubt they were grossly exaggerated, and we shall contrive to rub together very well."

"I am willing to try," he said, sending a challenging glance to Althea. He hugged his daughter close. "We shall doubtless be one happy little family."

The following morning Althea glared at Keswick's back as she cantered down the lane behind him and Meredith. The path was just wide enough for two horses, and she'd been forced to fall behind, with no other occupation than to listen to the nonsense he was telling the child.

The two of them burst into laughter. Keswick's deep-throated chuckle and Meredith's high giggle disturbed the stillness of the early morning, and Althea resented his presence anew. This was *her* special time with Meredith. She felt positive Keswick was behaving with unusual charm only to annoy her. Certainly he had never shown the slightest interest in the child before, and Althea was equally certain that he had never been so amusing or obliging with Deborah.

"Aunt Thea," Meredith called, twisting around in her saddle, "Papa said he used to ride here when he was a little boy, no bigger than me. And he used to always have his dog with him. Papa says he will get me a dog, too."

"Then I hope your papa is also willing to teach you how to care for a pet. It is a great deal of responsibility." Althea knew she sounded churlish and regretted her words the instant she saw Meredith's face. The child's smile wavered and her eyes, so like her father's, darkened suddenly with bewildered hurt.

"Not *such* a great deal, Merry," Keswick countered. "I think you will like taking care of your pup. Just make sure he is fed and kept brushed, and of course we must teach him to obey you. Perhaps we shall even teach him a trick or two."

"Really, Papa?"

He nodded and turned back to Althea. "Did you never have a dog when you were a child? Or a cat?"

The lane widened as they turned by the meadow, and Althea nudged her horse to come alongside Meredith's. "No, we did not," she answered shortly. "Uncle John did not hold with having animals in the house. A dog bit him once, I believe, and it rather soured him on having them about."

"A pity. I still remember a dog I had. I suppose I was about ten, and Barnabas was just about as big as me. And smart, too. I swear he understood every word I said."

"Assuredly, since you were on the same level."

Keswick grinned. "He was smarter than a lot of people I know."

"What happened to Barnabas, Papa?"

"I'm afraid he grew old and died, Merry, and I missed him dreadfully." He looked over the child's head at Althea and added, "I doubt you can understand the special closeness a child can develop with a pet since you never had one, but I do believe Merry would benefit if you allowed her a pup. I learned a lot from Barnabas."

"Yes, of course, and grew into such a sterling character. The benefits must be obvious to anyone."

"Why, thank you, Althea. I trust our plan meets with your approval then? I want to take Merry with me this morning and select a pup. You are welcome to come, if you would care to join us."

She glanced away from the look in his eyes. Keswick had always had the knack of making her feel in the wrong. Vexed with herself, she spoke sharply. "Thank you, but no. I ask only that you take responsibility for the creature, and please remember I should prefer not to have it in the drawing room. Of course, I realize I am here at your sufferance, and it is your house, but I hope you will have the courtesy to respect my feelings."

"Certainly, Althea, though I suspect when you see it you might change your mind. Did you never wish for a pet?"

He caught her unawares, and Althea found herself remembering the tiny white kitten she'd wanted as a child. "Once," she said rather wistfully. "A neighbor's cat had a litter, and I chanced to see them when we were visiting. There was one—just a tiny ball of white fur, with large blue eyes. When I held him, he curled up and went to sleep in my arms. I begged Aunt Emma to let me take it home,

14

but she would not permit me. Of course she had to consider my uncle's wishes."

"Oh, the poor little kitten," Meredith cried. "What happened to it, Aunt Thea?"

A shadow crossed Althea's eyes. She couldn't tell Meredith that the kittens had probably been drowned. She glanced at Keswick over the child's head. He knew what happened to unwanted cats. She was surprised and shaken by the sudden sympathy in his eyes.

"You could have a kitten now, Aunt Thea," Meredith consoled her, for she'd seldom heard Althea sound so sad.

"Do not be silly, Meredith. It was a long time ago, and I have no time for kittens now. What say we race to the big tree?"

Meredith spurred her pony, all thoughts of kittens and dogs vanishing as she raced ahead. Althea held her horse back, and Keswick, seeing what she was about, rode beside her. Meredith easily reached the tree before them and crowed in triumph. Althea couldn't help sharing a smile with Keswick. A truce of sorts was established, and the ride back to the house was almost pleasant. When they reached the narrow lane by the meadows, it was Meredith who rode ahead and Keswick cantered his black alongside Althea's mare.

"I will say this for you, my lord, your judgment of horseflesh is faultless. That's a beautiful stallion."

"What? Another compliment? Be careful, my dear, or you shall turn my head." He grinned, then turned to watch his daughter putting her pony through his paces. "I must admit you have done a splendid job with Meredith. She is entirely delightful."

"I can scarce take credit, my lord. Even though she has been much indulged, she is not at all spoiled. Meredith has a naturally sunny nature, and it seems to me she is exceptionally intelligent for a child her age."

"Of course she is. She *is* my daughter, you know," he teased, unable to resist provoking her.

"She may have her looks from you, Keswick, but I have little doubt her disposition and intelligence come from her mother."

"Shame on you, Althea! If you have an honest bone in your body, you will own that Deborah was a pretty widgeon. Merry, at least, is able to hold a conversation." He had only meant to tease her and cursed silently when he saw the sudden drawn look on her face.

Althea gave him no opportunity to say more. She urged her mare ahead and managed to ride into the stable yard beside Meredith. She had actually forgotten that Keswick was responsible for Deborah's death. Forgot, too, the one brief period when she'd found him undeniably attractive and charming— charming to the point where she'd nearly sided with him against her poor cousin.

Deborah had pleaded with Keswick to leave her alone at the manor until her child was born. Althea had thought it wrong of her cousin and told her so, but Keswick had left a few days later. Althea had missed him more than she had liked to admit. They had quarreled constantly but there was a vitality about the man that had made the old manor teem with excitement and energy. Once Keswick had left, even the air had seemed dull and lifeless and she'd blamed Deborah for driving him off. She'd had scant patience with the younger girl's megrims and

16

admonished her for being so weak. Deborah had died in child birth a month later. She had not had the will to live, the doctor had said. Althea had flayed herself with guilt, blaming both herself and Keswick.

Vowing she would not forget her cousin again, she strode into the house.

Keswick followed more slowly with Meredith, not unappreciative of the trim figure Althea presented in her blue riding habit. Not many women looked attractive from the rear in such garb, he thought, but she certainly did. Even more so than he'd remembered.

"Is Aunt Thea angry, Papa?"

"Not with you, darling. Only with herself, I think. You run along and change, and after breakfast we shall see about finding you a puppy."

Althea had little leisure to think about Keswick. She had taken refuge in her room after breakfast, but it wasn't long before Mrs. Pennington tapped on her door.

"Lady Penhallow is here, miss. Cheever put her in the blue drawing room and Miss Carlyle is with her, but she asked for you."

"I wondered how long it would take her to call. Tell her and Aunt Pysie I shall be down directly," Althea said with a smile for the housekeeper. She knew Mrs. Pennington shared her opinion of Lady Penhallow as the biggest gossip in the county.

When Althea entered the drawing room a few moments later, there was nothing in her demeanor to indicate anything but pleasure in receiving an unexpected visitor. She greeted the tall, heavyset woman pleasantly and begged her to be seated again.

"I can only stay for a moment, my dear. Gracious, I must have a hundred things to do today, but as I told my Fredrick, above all else I simply must bring dear Althea some of my strawberry preserves." She wagged a finger playfully in front of the younger woman. "Ah, you thought I forgot, but I remember you remarking how much you enjoyed them."

"How kind of you," Althea replied, although she could not recall ever expressing a preference for the preserves.

"Think nothing of it, my dear, but what is this I hear? Miss Carlyle has just been telling me that Keswick has returned and intends to take up residence here. I must say I was amazed, for I never thought to see him again. I understood he was quite settled abroad."

"Apparently not, although it is not so surprising he has returned, for Meredith is here." Althea smiled and wished she had something to occupy her idle hands. Lady Penhallow always made her feel restless.

"The poor child. How unsettling to suddenly have one's father appear out of nowhere. Is she terribly frightened of him?"

"No, of course not. Indeed, Meredith rode with him this morning, and now they are out searching the county for a suitable puppy for her."

"A puppy? How very odd, though I suppose he may have changed. I can only remember your dear cousin and how she seemed to go in terror of him. It must be distressing for you, Miss Underwood, and indeed for all of us, if it means we shall have Keswick back only to lose you."

"To lose me? I do not believe I quite understand, Lady Penhallow."

"Why, gracious me. I presumed you would not wish to remain here—not with Keswick in residence—and his aunt tells me that he means to take a wife. Surely, under the circumstances, you must feel yourself to be awkwardly placed, my dear."

Althea somehow managed a convincing laugh. "Goodness, Lady Penhallow, Keswick has only been home for two days. He scarcely has had time to meet anyone. Of course I hope he marries again, for Meredith's sake, but we are speaking of the future. I am sure there is no need to worry over it now."

"No, certainly not," Aunt Pysie added. "Andrew has been at pains to assure us that he does not wish to make any changes at present, and he realizes how very attached Meredith is to Althea."

"All the same, my dear, allow an older woman to give you the benefit of her advice. When Keswick marries again, you will find yourself in an odd position, you know, and I would be remiss in my duty if I did not advise you to begin planning now for your own future. You are still an attractive girl and there is no reason why you should not marry and establish your own home."

"Thank you, Lady Penhallow. I shall certainly consider your words, but you need not be concerned. My aunt Drucilla has asked me for years to make my home with her in London, and if it were not for Meredith, I would have done so. However, that is for the future. Now tell me, please, have you seen Mrs. Brubaker? Aunt Pysie told me yesterday the poor woman fell and hurt her back."

Lady Penhallow was successfully diverted, and she stayed with them another hour. Althea suspected that she prolonged her visit in hopes of seeing Keswick, but he did not return to the house until shortly after their visitor had left. He looked in on Althea as she was straightening the drawing room.

"Ah, sir, you arrived too late. Lady Penhallow just left, and she was most disappointed not to see you."

"How unfortunate I missed her. I saw the carriage, of course, but not wishing to encroach upon your guests, I discreetly remained in the stables with Merry until your visitor took her leave."

"Beast! Encroach upon my guests, indeed! How can you say such a thing when you know full well it was you she wished to see?"

"But I did not wish to see her," he said, and grinned, quite unrepentant. "Will you come out to the stables and see Merry's puppy? She has, so far, changed his name six times. At present, it is Buttons because she says his eyes look like shiny black buttons."

Althea was hard put not to return his smile, but remembering her promise to herself, she replied curtly, "Thank you, my lord, but I've no desire to see the animal. Now if you will excuse me, please?"

Sweeping up the stairs, she told herself that any desire to go to the stables and play with a silly puppy was childish and quite beneath her dignity. She was nearly convinced of the truth of her words when she entered her room. She paused inside the door. A large white wicker basket sat on the windowseat. Curious, she crossed the room and was about to reach for the basket when she heard a tiny cry. Quickly, she flipped open the lid and lifted out a tiny white kitten.

It barely weighed a pound and fit easily in her hand. Althea held it close, rubbing its small head and smiling foolishly as it opened its blue eyes. A small pink tongue darted out to lick her hand. Holding the kitten carefully, she sat down on the windowseat and looked into the basket. She slowly drew out the card.

Chapter 2

Althea read the scrawled message while the kitten alternately batted at it and tried to sink its sharp little teeth into the corner of the note. *Be careful, Althea—this female has not yet learned to sheath her claws.* The brief warning appeared on the reverse side of one of Keswick's calling cards.

Althea laid the note aside and held the tiny bundle of fur against her chest. The kitten was so helpless and so very trusting, but she could not keep it. Looking into the animal's round blue eyes, she told herself again that, she could not possibly keep it. Accepting such a gift would put her under an obligation to Keswick. She wished he had not done anything so . . . kind. Resolutely, she returned both the kitten and the card to the wicker basket and, carrying it carefully, went in search of Keswick. He was not in the library or any of the drawing rooms, and she finally inquired of Cheever if he had seen his lordship.

"The earl gave me to understand he'd be visiting some of his tenants, Miss Underwood. I do not believe it is his intention to return before late afternoon."

A plaintive mew from the basket startled the

butler and Althea stifled a smile. "Please have Mary bring a saucer of milk to my room, Cheever. And if Lord Keswick should return sooner, see that I am informed."

It was just like the man to saddle her with an animal and then disappear, Althea thought. However, she couldn't hold the kitten to blame and it was undoubtedly hungry. She returned to her room and, unable to resist, freed the tiny creature from its basket. When Mary tapped on the door a short time later, she found her mistress playing with the kitten on the rug beneath the windows.

"Why, miss, I couldn't think what you'd be wanting with a saucer of milk, but now I see. What a cute little thing. Wherever did you find her?"

"This creature belongs to the earl, Mary, and although I do not know a great deal about cats, I believe you have the wrong gender."

"Pardon, miss?"

"The wrong sex, Mary. It appears the kitten is a male. Set the dish down here and we shall see if he will drink from it."

The kitten proved eager for the milk and in his haste almost upset the dish. Both of his front paws ended up in the saucer, and the two women watched with amusement. When the dish was lapped dry, the kitten turned his attention to his paws and licked them clean, too.

"Well, he was right hungry, wasn't he, miss?" Just a baby yet, I should think, not above seven or eight weeks."

"Do you know much about cats, Mary?"

"Depends on how you mean, Miss Underwood. I've been around 'em all my life. I can't recollect a time when we didn't have a passel of cats in the house."

"Excellent. Then you will undoubtedly know how to set about training him. Consider it one of your prime duties from now on, or at least until the earl returns."

Althea had every intention of returning the kitten, but her resolve weakened considerably as the day passed. Which was probably just what Keswick intended, she thought, and the reason he'd stayed clear of the house. She tried ignoring the little imp. The kitten, however, with much good sense, batted and teased at her skirt until she picked him up. Once settled comfortably in her lap, he curled into a ball and went contentedly to sleep.

When she rose at last, Althea placed the bundle of fur on the cushioned windowseat. A moment later she hastily rescued the creature as he stumbled off the seat in an effort to follow her.

"Very well," she said, holding the kitten up in front of her face. "You may come with me this time, but if Keswick is back, I shall deposit you in *his* lap, and I hope you may scratch him."

Keswick was indeed back and in the drawing room. So were Aunt Pysie, Meredith, and her governess, Miss Appletree. Althea stood in the doorway for a moment, quietly watching them. None of the four noticed her entrance, for they were all absorbed in the antics of a small puppy, which was rapidly destroying a ball of yarn.

Keswick was the first to see her and rose at once. "Althea, I do apologize. I told Merry she must keep her pup in the kitchen, but apparently she neglected to shut the door and he followed her in here."

"Of course, my lord, and it is obvious you were making every effort to remove it."

"Aunt Thea, he is such a little puppy to be left all alone in the kitchen. Can he not stay, just this once, please?"

"I hardly think being left in the care of a chef, two assistant cooks, and numerous scullery maids qualifies as being alone, Meredith," she said, but she was smiling and the child grinned up at her.

"It would be only fair," Keswick drawled. "I see you brought your own pet down with you."

"My pet, sir? You left this creature in my room and then disappeared so I could not return it. I will have you know, I spent the better part of the day in a vain effort to prevent it from destroying my room." Her words did not carry quite the sting she desired. The kitten, apparently fascinated by her moving lips, stretched his paw up to bat gently at them.

"Aunt Thea, she's trying to tell you to be quiet." Meredith giggled.

"She is a *he*," Althea said, catching at the paws. "And since you, my lord, are so adept at handling animals, you may have him back."

Keswick instantly folded his arms behind his back. "Oh, no. I can handle dogs and horses, but cats dislike me. The creature scratched me twice this morning. If you really do not wish to keep him, Althea, I shall return him to the farm tonight." He glanced at his daughter and added quietly, "Of course you know what Dutton will do with him."

The kitten mewed in protest, and Althea, knowing she could not allow him to be drowned, gave up the battle. Taking her seat, she addressed Aunt Pysie. "Would you pour me a cup of tea, please? I

25

feel in need of a restorative. I hope you realize now
how treacherous your nephew is, ma'am."

"Treacherous? Well, I would not say—"

"He sat in this very room and assured us he
would not overset my arrangements, and now he
has introduced a dog and a cat into our drawing
room. I shudder to think what he may next contrive." She glanced down at the kitten in her lap.
Wide awake now, he eyed the puppy curiously.
Althea set him down and they all watched as he
arched his tiny back and approached the pup warily.

"If that is all," Aunt Pysie was saying, "you need
not be concerned. Why, when I recall some of the
tricks he got up to as a boy—do you remember, Andrew, the time you and that scamp, young Jack
Filmore, induced the circus man to release his bear
in the stable yard? Lord Walpole was visiting us,
and when he went out to ride and saw that bear,
gracious, I was certain he was going to suffer a
stroke."

"A bear? Did you really, Papa?"

"Thank you for telling us, Aunt Pysie. I can
clearly see now that I have been kindly treated,"
Althea said.

"It was a tame bear," Keswick protested, but he
laughed at the memory.

"Which, of course, makes all the difference,"
Althea observed.

"It did to old Walpole, but I give you my word I
have outgrown such pranks. It was most unkind of
Aunt Pysie to recall the incident." To Meredith he
added, "I was beaten severely for that trick, young
lady, as I deserved to be."

Miss Appletree, who had been won over instantly

by Keswick's lack of condescension and his easy manners, nodded her approval. "I'm certain most young boys get up to such pranks now and then and may be forgiven their high spirits."

"I wonder if Lord Walpole shares your views," Althea murmured softly.

They were interrupted by Cheever. He tapped lightly on the door and then opened it to announce the arrival of Mr. George Selwyn.

The young man who entered was neither a member of the dandy set nor of the more sporting Corinthians, but fell somewhere in between the two. He was dressed for riding in a drab olive coat but sported a short green and white waistcoat beneath it. His fawn kerseymere breeches were nothing remarkable, but his glossy brown topboots were adorned with tassels. There were many who considered his blond curls and brows over clear blue eyes to be a handsome combination, and Althea was among their number.

"Mr. Selwyn, how delightful of you to call." She rose, gave him her hand in greeting, and then turned to stand beside him. "You do, of course, recall your cousin?"

"Of course." He smiled and extended his hand. "Welcome home, Keswick. Lady Penhallow told me you had returned." He bent to bestow a kiss on his aunt, gave a brief nod of acknowledgment to Miss Appletree, and patted Meredith on the head.

Althea indicated that he should sit beside her on the sofa and at once poured him a cup of tea. "I fear you find us a trifle disordered this afternoon. Keswick has given Meredith a puppy and gifted me with a kitten."

"I confess I was somewhat surprised when I entered, for I have never known you to allow animals in the drawing room before. I should have guessed it was my cousin's doing."

"It was," Keswick agreed. "I was explaining to Miss Underwood my belief that a child benefits from having a pet. But as I recall, you never much cared for animals, did you, Selwyn?"

"Not as housepets, certainly. I do have a fine kennel of hunting dogs, and I believe there are any number of cats in the stables." He eyed the kitten and the pup on the floor distastefully.

"Having never had pets, I remain undecided," Althea said, and bent down to scoop up the kitten. "But you will have to own, George, this is a handsome little creature, and I mean to see he is taught proper manners."

"The kitten certainly makes a pretty picture held in your arms, Althea. Almost I could envy it."

Aunt Pysie cleared her throat, and Keswick made some sort of derisive sound. The puppy, deprived of its playmate, eyed the tassels swinging from George's boots and, with a sudden lunge, attacked them.

The movement startled George. He spilled his tea and the hot liquid seeped through his breeches, scalding his skin. He jumped up, inadvertently kicked the pup, and swabbed at the rapidly spreading stain. The little dog yelped and, with tail between his legs, scuttled across the room to hide beneath Keswick's chair.

"Oh, George, I am dreadfully sorry," Althea said, handing him a cloth. "Has the tea burned you?"

"Careless of you, cousin," Keswick drawled, a look of contempt in his eyes. "Did that small pup frighten you?"

Meredith did not need the warning glance from Miss Appletree to hurriedly retrieve her pet. In truth, she was more concerned about the pup than their guest and sheltered him in her arms. She shot George a resentful look. "He was only playing with your old tassels."

"Lady Meredith!" Miss Appletree breathed.

"Apologize to Mr. Selwyn at once, Meredith, and then you may go to your room," Althea scolded.

"Yes, Aunt Thea. I am sorry, Mr. Selwyn," Meredith mouthed dutifully, but her dark eyes continued to glare at him and Miss Appletree hastily ushered her from the room.

"Pray excuse me for a moment," Althea said, and followed them out the door. When she returned, she was without the kitten. She apologized again to George, although he hastened to reassure her that no real harm had been done.

She resumed her seat, but the conversation that followed was stilted. Aunt Pysie remained unnaturally quiet and a distinct animosity flared between the two gentlemen. While Althea was accustomed to conversing at length with George Selwyn, for he was a frequent caller, she found it difficult to do so under Keswick's eyes. A quarter hour passed slowly and she felt considerably relieved when George at last rose to depart.

Believing she owed him some extraordinary civility, Althea linked her arm in his and walked with him to the door. "I apologize again, George, for the upset, and I promise the next time you call there will be no animals in the drawing room."

"You have nothing to apologize for, my dear Althea. It was, after all, an accident. I only hope I did not harm Meredith's pup. Please convey my apologies to her."

"I shall, but she should never have spoken to you in such a manner. I fear she has been over excited since her papa came home."

"I knew Keswick's return would cause an upheaval, although I had not quite envisioned this result," he replied with a smile, and gestured toward the stain on his breeches.

"George, I apologize again—"

"There is no need, my dear. This is nothing, but I am concerned with the other changes my cousin's return will entail. I had hoped we might have a moment in private to discuss it. Have you formed any plans?"

"Plans?"

They paused in the entry hall, and George turned her to face him, retaining her hand in his own. His blue eyes were serious as he stared down at her. "You may be perfectly frank with me, my dear. Keswick may be my cousin, but I hold no illusions about the man, and his return has certainly placed you in a most awkward situation."

"A bit uncomfortable, perhaps, but no more than that. Keswick is doing his best to be accommodating, and Aunt Pysie is here to maintain the proprieties," she said, and smiled to reassure him.

"Surely you do not intend to remain here?"

"I see no reason to run away—Keswick will not eat me, you know. This has been my home for the last five years, George, and even if I did desire to remove from here, there is Meredith to consider."

"She has her papa home to look after her. There is no need for you to sacrifice yourself any longer."

"I do not consider looking after Meredith to be a

sacrifice. Indeed, I love her dearly, and except for Aunt Drucilla, she is all I have left of my family."

"But if Keswick marries again? Lady Penhallow told me it is his intention. What will you do then?"

"I shall cross that bridge when we come to it," Althea said, making an effort to sound unconcerned. She added with laugh, "A great deal will depend on the lady whom he marries."

"Tell me the truth, Althea. Do you stay here only because there is nowhere else for you to go and be comfortable?"

"No, of course not. Do get that notion out of your head, George. I stay because I choose to. If it should become uncomfortable for me, I may always remove to my aunt's house in London."

"You have yet another option, Althea, though I hesitate to remind you. I know I promised you I would not speak of it again, but—"

"And I beg you will keep your promise, sir. Dear George, we are such good friends, pray do not spoil it. I *cannot* consider marriage just now—" She broke off abruptly as Keswick entered the hall.

"Oh, are you still here, Selwyn?"

"I was just leaving, cousin."

Self-consciously, Althea withdrew her hands and stepped away. Selwyn waited for a moment, hoping Keswick would take himself off, but his cousin lounged against the door, an interested observer.

"I shall say good day, Althea, but I hope you will remember what I have said."

"I shall, George, and thank you."

Althea turned, and though Keswick said not a word, his dark eyes were brimful of laughter. She snapped at him, "Am I to be permitted no privacy with my callers, my lord?"

"Ah, did I interrupt a tender moment, my dear? I rather thought I was effecting a rescue." Keswick stood tall and straight, towering over her.

Althea wished he was not quite so tall, not quite so much a *man*. He somehow made other men seem less substantial. She understood how Deborah, dear sensitive, shy Deborah, had frequently been intimidated.

"I doubt I would ever need rescuing from your cousin, my lord. *He* is a gentleman in every sense of the word."

"And I am not? Well, I will not argue on that head. If I apologize, will you come out to the stables with me? I wish your opinion of a mare I bought this morning."

"Thank you, Keswick, but if you do not object, I shall see her later. At present I want a word with Meredith about her conduct."

"Don't be too hard on her, will you? Selwyn did kick her pup."

"But not intentionally, and it certainly does not excuse her bad manners," she replied, but she spoke to his back. Keswick had already retreated down the hall. Exasperated, she climbed the stairs to the nursery.

Miss Appletree met her at the door. The governess was an older woman, of good family, and Althea had engaged her for two reasons. One was her obvious intelligence; the other, the assurance that the somewhat stern spinster would not overindulge Meredith. Time had proven her correct in her judgment, but now Miss Appletree echoed Keswick's words.

"I realize Lady Meredith was rude, Miss Underwood, but perhaps there was some slight provocation. Mr. Selwyn did kick her pup, although I am certain it was not deliberate."

"No, of course not. I fear the puppy startled him. He is not accustomed to having dogs or cats in the house," Althea said, watching Meredith as she played in the far corner of the room.

"Is it not amazing how animals and children either take to a person or not? It is my belief that they are able to see through the veneer of civilized manners to the true character beneath."

Althea had known for some time that Miss Appletree did not quite approve of George Selwyn and she eyed her speculatively before commenting. "There are some people, myself included, who do not approve of animals in the household, Miss Appletree. I hope you do not mean to imply that my character is somehow lacking?"

"Gracious, no. Why, anyone with half an eye could see how the kitten took to you. No, no, Miss Underwood, I spoke in general."

Trumped and double-trumped, Althea thought. She knew she would not get the better of Miss Appletree and retreated strategically.

A compromise of sorts was reached. The animals were allowed the run of the house most of the time but were not permitted in the drawing room whenever guests were present. Althea, for all her supposed disdain for the pup, was seen by the servants on several occasions to stoop and fondle him. As for the white kitten, now christened Mr. Bows, he followed his mistress about the house in much the same manner that Buttons followed Lady Meredith. Not for the world would Althea acknowledge the comfort she found in the tiny white ball of fur.

33

He curled upon her pillow in the evenings, and Althea even found herself holding ridiculous conversations with the kitten.

The summer days passed pleasantly and a state of harmony seemed to prevail at Keswick Manor. Nothing occurred to disturb the tranquil routine of the days until Lady Penhallow's dinner. Of course, speculation about the earl's return had been rife in the neighborhood, and several persons had called, but Keswick had eluded them all. He was seldom in the house during the day, and their curiosity went unsatisfied. Lady Penhallow herself called three times without once catching sight of the earl. Acting on the belief that he could not refuse her, the lady issued an invitation to a dinner honoring his return to the community.

Keswick thought otherwise and told Althea so during breakfast on Thursday morning. "Give her my apologies. Tell her I have a previous engagement or something."

"Impossible, my lord. If you had any sort of engagement with anyone in the county, you may be certain Lady Penhallow would know of it. You cannot mean to insult her."

"Can I not?" he asked, his brows lifting, and gave her a quizzical smile.

"No. She would be mortally offended, and you cannot wish to be on bad terms with your neighbors."

"And even if you wish to, Andrew," Aunt Pysie said between bites of a scone heavily lathered with preserves, "which anyone might understand with a neighbor like Lady Penhallow, you could not be so uncivil as to own it. I myself have frequently wished she would not concern herself so readily in our affairs, but not for a moment would I consider offending her. To be at outs with one's neighbors would be so very unpleasant. Although I recollect the time last Christmas when she insisted on showing me the proper way to prepare snuff—as if I would ever take snuff—I own I was sorely tempted to set her straight. But not a word did I say. It simply would not do."

"And you were very right, Aunt Pysie," Althea said with a dark look in Keswick's direction.

"I believe I still have the recipe somewhere about, not that I would use it, for I did let George try it and he said it was far too heavily scented, which indeed was my own opinion. Not that I am any judge of such matters. Andrew, if you would care to—"

"Thank you, Aunt Pysie, but no. I have my own sort put up by Lord Wrexham."

"Yes, naturally, most gentlemen do. Which just proves my point." She nodded and helped herself to another scone.

"What was your point, Aunt Pysie?" Althea asked, and wondered what new diet permitted five scones drenched in butter and preserves.

"Why, that one must be civil, of course. Gracious, Althea, I thought you would understand that at once."

"I certainly did," Keswick said, returning from the sideboard with a platter of eggs and kippers. He offered it to his aunt, but she waved him away.

"None for me, thank you, Andrew. I shall just nibble on these few scones with my tea. One must watch one's weight."

Keswick offered the dish to Althea, but she, too, declined and watched while he served himself a brimming plate. The chef was delighted to have the earl back in residence, for Keswick was a man who ate with considerable relish. Indeed, Althea thought, observing him, it was a wonder he was not obese, considering the amount of food he consumed. She tried to picture him as he might look in his old age, with a large, rounded belly and a foot propped up, swollen from gout. The image was ludicrous, and her brown eyes lit with suppressed laughter.

The earl looked across at her, wondering what had put the sparkle in her eyes. He thought, not for the first time, that when Althea relaxed her guard, she was rather beautiful.

"Are we agreed then?" she asked, glancing away from his probing eyes.

"Agreed on what?"

"On accepting Lady Penhallow's dinner invitation for tomorrow evening. I thought you said you understood Aunt Pysie's point."

"Certainly I understood her, but what has that to say to anything? Surely there must be some way of refusing Lady Penhallow without offending her."

Althea shook her head. "Not unless you were to become seriously ill, and then, no doubt, she would feel compelled to come and dose you with one of her special restoratives."

"Lord, spare me that. All right, I concede. Accept the invitation, but I give you both fair warning. Do not dare leave me alone with her for above five minutes, or I will not be responsible for what this wicked tongue of mine might say."

Althea laughed, although she knew he was speaking only partly in jest. Keswick had always scorned the conventions and what he termed "polite society." It was that sort of irreverent attitude that had earned him an abominable reputation.

The earl, however, was apparently on his best behavior the following evening. Althea descended the stairs and saw him waiting for her in the great hall. She had ample time to observe him as she came down the long, curved stairs. Keswick had chosen a dark blue tailcoat, its high collar and lapels trimmed in black velvet, which, Althea admitted, fit him to perfection, as did his black satin pantaloons and blue-striped silk stockings. He looked every inch the proper country gentleman and she graciously told him so when she gave him her hand in greeting.

"No matter what Lady Penhallow may find to say about your manners, she will not be able to fault your dress, my lord."

"Thank you, Althea, and may I return the compliment. You are looking charmingly. Never tell me you had that gown made up in the country."

She dimpled, her eyes full of mischief. "La, sir, your knowledge of feminine apparel is amazing. Aunt Drucilla sent this from London. How clever of you to recognize it," she teased, fingering the yellow silk with its daring low neckline.

"Let me see, child," Aunt Pysie said, rising from the sofa. "That color is most becoming to you. Very pretty, indeed. Well, I always did say Drucilla Rowley had excellent taste, but it seems a shame to waste such finery on Lady Penhallow. I wonder who else she has invited."

Althea gathered her gold Kashmir shawl closer about her shoulders and made certain the black ribbons, which tied beneath the high waist, were not tangled. "You may be certain she has asked everyone of note in the county. George told me she intends to sit thirty down to dinner."

"Trust George to know. He always did cater to the old lady. Some distant connection, I believe. I daresay he still visits her once a week," Keswick said calmly enough, but there was an odd light in his eyes. "When did you see my cousin, Althea?"

"He called yesterday to bring us the latest *Gazette*. He subscribes to it, you know, and is beforehand with all the news."

"I believe you were out with Meredith, Andrew, when George drove over with the paper," Aunt Pysie told him. "It was full of the Regent's appalling behavior with Lady Fitzherbert, and I must say we spent a very pleasant hour or two discussing it. Indeed, you may say what you will about Prinny, but without the scandals he and his brothers create, one wonders what there would be to talk about."

"I am sure you would find something, Aunt," he replied absently, ushering the ladies to the door. "Obviously I have been remiss in my duties as a host. I did not realize you were dependent on a neighbor for news from London. I shall enter a subscription to the *Gazette* for you tomorrow, Althea, and you may tell George that it is no longer necessary for him to drive over merely to lend you his paper."

Aunt Pysie tittered and tapped Keswick's arm with her fan. "Dear Andrew, pray do not be so foolish. Only a blind man would suppose that is the reason George spends so much time here. And you surely would not wish to deprive either Althea or your cousin of the pleasure they take in each other's company. I have been expecting an announcement anytime this last year. Ah, it reminds me of the time Sir Arnold courted me. The excuses he used to contrive to pay me a call—it still puts me to the blush." She continued to chatter as Keswick helped her into the carriage, unmindful of the effect of her words.

The earl had a hard look in his eyes, and his jaw seemed tight with the effort to control himself. Althea knew not where to look and sat, blushing, in the darkness of the carriage.

Chapter 3

The drive to Lady Penhallow's was accomplished
in less than thirty minutes, but it seemed an eternity to Althea. Neither she nor Keswick uttered a
word or paid any attention to Aunt Pysie's rambling monologue. The earl stared straight ahead
and Althea imagined she could feel the anger radiating from him. He disliked his cousin and had
made it clear he resented her friendship with
George. Now Aunt Pysie had put the ridiculous notion in his head that it was something more than
mere friendship.

Althea fumed. The situation was impossible. She
could not tell Keswick that his cousin had proposed
on numerous occasions and she'd refused his offers.
To do so would place her beyond the pale, for no
lady flaunted a gentleman's offer. Yet she must
somehow contrive to set Keswick straight or he
might not agree to her plans.

Althea intended to remove to London when
Keswick wed and she wanted to take Meredith
with her. It was the only possible solution. The earl
would marry, and soon. Althea held no illusions on
that head. One could not deny that he was handsome, wealthy, and titled. Many ladies would willingly disregard his past when they weighed it

against the prospect of becoming a countess. Indeed, Althea thought, she could easily name a half-dozen females who would be ecstatic at the opportunity. Unfortunately, none of them were suitable as a mother for Meredith.

Althea believed Keswick would agree to her plan. After all, he'd been parted from his daughter for five years and hardly knew the child. When he married, he would naturally be preoccupied with his new wife and the lady would, no doubt, lend her support to Althea's scheme.

It was an ideal solution for everyone, or it had been until Aunt Pysie's ill-timed words. Althea knew Keswick harbored an irrational jealousy of his cousin, and there was no reasoning with him on the subject. If he thought she intended to wed George, he would never agree to give her charge of Meredith. Althea stole a look at his stony countenance. She *must* find the words to convince him of the truth.

Keswick, however, gave her little opportunity. He assisted her from the carriage with his usual air of unconcern and escorted both ladies to the door. Just before the butler admitted them, he whispered to Althea, "I believe it will cause less talk if I do not appear to pay you any undue attention."

Althea glanced up at his arrogant profile. Keswick was going to be difficult. She had no chance to reply as they silently followed the butler up the broad stairs and entered a large salon.

Lady Penhallow greeted the party effusively while her husband murmured a few words in his usual quiet manner. The viscount was a small man, of gentle nature and scholarly bent. Althea enjoyed conversing with him but was seldom granted the opportunity when the more domineering Lady Penhallow was present. This occasion proved no different. She'd spoken no more than a few words to Lord Penhallow before she found herself quickly surrounded by a number of ladies of her acquaintance. Keswick, she noticed, was pulled off into a corner of the room by several young bucks, apparently anxious for the chance to question a known rake.

Elizabeth Fielding, the elder daughter of Sir Edward and Lady Fielding, tapped Althea playfully on the arm. "La, my dear, I had no notion he was so handsome. Small wonder you have been hiding him."

"Pay no attention to her," Edith, the younger Fielding sister, remarked. "Lizzie thinks any creature with two good legs is handsome. Mama said it is far more likely you find it excessively uncomfortable living in the same house as *him*."

"I fear you are both wrong," Althea replied, forcing her lips into a smile. "I gather you *are* referring to the earl? We are related by marriage, you know, and I find him neither extraordinarily handsome nor uncomfortable. We are certainly civil to each other, but he is gone a great deal of the time, so I scarcely see him."

"Doing it too brown or else you must be blind," Elizabeth said, her gaze devouring the earl from across the room. "Only look at those broad shoulders and his smoldering eyes. I vow he gives me chills."

"Then I suggest you adjust your shawl," Lucinda Deerborn drawled, linking her arm in Althea's. "And try reading something other than those dreadful penny novels. You are beginning to sound like one."

"Jealous, Lucinda? At least *I* know what it is like to be totally enslaved by love's passion," Elizabeth retorted sharply before dragging her sister off with her.

"Why, that little cat. It is a wonder someone has not yet strangled her. Just because Captain Hewlitt was foolish enough to take her out driving a few times, she imagines herself to be in the throes of some grand romance—and the rest of us green with envy."

"Pay her no heed," Althea advised with a real smile that grew into a laugh. "Enslaved by love's passion, indeed! Have you ever heard such nonsense? We must pray Lady Fielding succeeds in seeing Lizzie safely wed before the girl's imagination leads her to commit an unforgivable indiscretion."

"Like throwing herself at Keswick? Look at her, Thea. I have seldom seen a more brazen display."

They watched Elizabeth edge into the crowd of young men surrounding the earl. She maneuvered into a position next to him and clung to his arm. Keswick bent his head, apparently whispering something to the girl, and they clearly heard her shrill laugh ring out.

"If she chooses to throw out lures to Keswick, she may get more than she bargained for," Althea said tartly. She turned her back on the pair and moved to a sofa near the fireplace.

"Gracious, Thea, you cannot believe he would pay any attention to a girl just out of the schoolroom?" Lucinda glanced back over her shoulder at the couple before seating herself beside her friend.

"Keswick certainly does not appear to be discouraging her, and do not forget Deborah was just seventeen when he wed her."

"An arranged marriage, and a disastrous one at that. Of course, Lord Keswick was younger then, too, but from what I have heard he now prefers a more sophisticated lady. Tell me, my dear, while we have a moment alone, how does he treat you?"

"Oh, Lucy, not you, too! I swear everyone in the county is busy speculating about his return. Half have me married off to him and the other half believes he shall ravish me, or something equally dreadful."

"I wonder what it would be like to be ravished by him. Quite enjoyable, I should think."

"Lucinda!"

Lucinda chuckled and was on the verge of offering an apology when she caught sight of a young man across the room. She grabbed Althea's hand and whispered urgently, "Gracious, look. Richard Kingsly just came in. I vow I am amazed Lady Penhallow invited him. Everyone knows he positively loathes Keswick."

"I am not—it is precisely the sort of thing she *would* do," Althea said, her eyes following Kingsly. He was several years her junior, of slight build, with sandy-brown hair and piercing blue eyes. He had been passionately devoted to her cousin and furious when Althea's uncle had given his consent to Deborah's match with the earl.

"He was absolutely crushed when Deborah died," Lucinda said, echoing her thoughts. "And judging by the way he's glaring at Keswick, I doubt he has yet forgiven him. Do you think he means to call him out?"

"On what grounds? The idea is absurd. Keswick was not even here when Deborah died," Althea said, a shadow passing across her eyes. It was still difficult for her to speak of her cousin's death, but she added conscientiously, "You know as well as I do the doctor said no one was to blame."

"Are you defending him? I can scarce believe my ears. I remember how distraught you were when Deborah died, and I know you blamed Keswick. Why, you said—"

"I said a great many foolish things. Pray do not repeat them, Lucy. I was so full of grief, I had to blame someone. It seemed so unfair, so unjust that she should die so young. You can have no notion of how helpless it makes one feel. You want to strike out at someone, anyone, and Keswick was easy to blame. If Deb had been more content in her marriage. . . But Dr. Mayhew told me he doubted it would have made a difference."

"You have forgiven Keswick then?"

"I . . . I try not to hold him responsible. It does no good to nourish grudges, you know, and it is all in the past now."

"Perhaps you should tell Richard Kingsly so. He looks positively vengeful, and I have heard him say on more than one occasion that had he been allowed to wed Deborah, she would still be alive."

"Yes, and how conveniently he forgets my cousin had no wish to wed him. Oh, she liked him well enough, but a younger son with no prospects . . . I doubt she would have accepted Kingsly on any terms."

George Selwyn, Timothy Ormsby, and Peter Farnsworth put an end to the ladies' private conversation. The three gentlemen crowded around them and reported rumors of an impromptu dance after dinner. Both Timothy and Peter teased Lucinda for a dance, and under cover of their noisy banter George drew a chair near and spoke quietly to Althea.

"I hope you will not take it amiss, my dear, if I drop a word of warning in your ear. There has been so much talk about Keswick's return, I believe you would be ill advised to stand up with him. Your name has been linked with his several times this evening, and I know you would not wish to encourage such talk."

"Thank you, George. It is humbling to realize how little faith my friends have in my character. You are not the first to warn me, and I feel certain you will not be the last."

She spoke so calmly, and in such an even tone, that it took a moment for her meaning to penetrate.

"Althea, you are assuredly mistaken. Your character is not in question, not at all, my dear. Of course your friends are concerned, but consider Keswick's reputation. Given his past and the fact that you have led a rather sheltered life, it is small wonder if we who cherish you express a measure of concern."

"Your concern is apparently misplaced, George." She would not do anything so vulgar as to point, but Althea nodded in the direction of the earl. "I am unacquainted with the young lady, but Keswick has been exerting his charm on her behalf for the last quarter hour."

George glanced across the room. His eyes narrowed with contempt and a cynical smile twisted his lips. "Regina Montague. Birds of a feather and all that, I suppose."

"I trust you mean to enlighten me, sir. Who is she and what has she done to earn your disapproval?"

"She is Emma Harding's niece, and the *on-dit* is she was sent to her aunt after kicking up a scandal in London. I don't know all the particulars, but her name was linked with Lord Ashcroft."

"Gracious, she had best have a care or her reputation will be in tatters," Althea said, studying the slender blonde. She wore an extremely low-cut blue silk, which clung to her body. It was entirely unsuitable for a young girl, and Althea judged that Miss Montague could not be a day above eighteen. Still, the girl did the dress justice.

"I doubt the lady cares," George was saying. "I met her the other day at Lady Fielding's and she made it abundantly clear she wishes to have nothing to do with us poor provincials. She finds it a dead bore here."

"Well, she certainly does not appear bored now."

"No, nor does Keswick. As I said, birds of a feather . . . I have no doubt her lack of breeding meets with his full approval."

Althea doubted Keswick was concerned with the lady's manners or lack of them. He was too engrossed with the plunging neckline of her gown and the artful way the girl was plying her fan. Althea said nothing, however, and the dinner gong sounded before George could comment further.

There were, as George had predicted, at least thirty guests sitting down to dinner. Althea looked down the length of the table to where Keswick sat between Lady Penhallow and Mrs. Harding and smothered a smile. It was going to be a very lengthy dinner. Miss Montague, with whom the earl might have amused himself, was too far down the table to converse with him. And Sir Edward and Lord Penhallow, both of whom he liked tolerably well, graced the far end of the table. She would own herself surprised if Keswick managed to finish the dinner without insulting his hostess.

In that she wronged the earl. The conversation may not have been the sort of repartee in which he delighted, but there was much in Lady Penhallow's artless chatter to amuse him silently and the food was excellent. Indeed, he had seldom sat down to a more elaborate meal. They were served semelles of carp, heavily seasoned, removed with a fillet of succulent veal. Quails and ducklings followed with cauliflowers, green beans, and peas, and just as Keswick felt he could not eat another bite, dressed lobster was served with fresh asparagus. Lady Penhallow urged him to just sample it, for her chef was renown for his skill with lobster and would be mortally offended if Keswick refused it.

Althea, with the advantage of having dined with the Penhallows before, took only a small portion of the main dishes offered and finished her dinner with a small plate of strawberries and cream. Miss Montague, she noticed, had eaten heavily of the first two removes and now seemed to be sulking as the interminable dinner continued. Since she was seated between Peter Farnsworth and Richard Kingsly, she might have been the center of attention. However, she disdained both those gentlemen's attempts to engage her in conversation and so, with no one to converse with, sat staring moodily down the table at the earl. Althea saw Kingsly glance at Miss Montague and then at the earl. It was not a pleasant look and she felt uneasy. She hoped Kingsly did not intend to make a scene.

Lady Penhallow rose at last, signaling to the other ladies to follow her. They withdrew into a large drawing room, where she collapsed heavily against the plump cushions on a blue sofa. She fanned herself languidly and motioned for Althea to attend her.

"Tell me, my dear, do you think Keswick enjoyed his dinner? I particularly wished to please him as this is his first engagement since his return. If he enjoys himself, we might persuade him to venture out more, and you, too, of course. It seems we have barely caught sight of you since his return."

"Keswick would be hard to please indeed if he found fault with your dinner. It was a feast worthy of the Regent," Althea answered diplomatically, ignoring the latter part of Lady Penhallow's comments. The woman reminded her of a cat toying with its prey.

"And you, Althea? Are you enjoying yourself? I invited all the young men in the county, but as you well know, there are not many of an age to interest you. Selwyn, of course, but excepting him the only bachelor in our company is Keswick."

"I promise you I am quite content. Mr. Selwyn is always excellent company, and it is delightful to see Lucinda Deerborn and Lady Fielding again. It does seem an age since I have paid any calls, but then our inclement weather discourages visiting overmuch, does it not?"

Lady Penhallow smiled even while she fumed with inner frustration. Althea Underwood refused to be drawn into commenting on either the earl or

Selwyn. Her tiny gray eyes studied the girl before she changed tactics abruptly.

"I have engaged some musicians to play for us shortly—just some country dances, you know. I fear you might lack for partners, but at least dear Keswick will not. Did you see how Miss Montague was flirting with him? And Elizabeth Fielding's manners must put her mother to the blush. She practically threw herself at him."

"I am certain Keswick must be flattered beyond measure," Althea replied dryly. She was saved from further comment as Pysie Carlyle and Lucinda Deerborn joined them.

"Dear me, such a dinner," Aunt Pysie said, settling herself on the sofa next to Lady Penhallow. "I shall have to eat biscuits for a week and there is nothing I loathe more. Those strawberries were quite delicious—were they from your greenhouse? And you must promise to give me the chef's recipe for the carp, which was truly excellent."

Althea took advantage of Aunt Pysie's presence to escape. She drew Lucinda into an alcove with her, saying softly, "The crown should employ Lady Penhallow as a spy, for I have never met a more determined inquisitor."

"Has she been grilling you? I think it is her main joy in life. She simply must know everything about everyone in Cumberland. I would wager it is the reason her daughter moved so far away."

"I should not be surprised. I hope she has the brass to tackle Keswick directly. She would be well served if he gave her one of his infamous setdowns."

"Did I hear you mention Lord Keswick?" Regina

Montague asked with a sly smile as she joined them.

"Miss Underwood was just saying she hoped his lordship would enjoy the evening," Lucinda answered glibly.

"Oh." Regina turned wide green eyes on Althea and looked down at her with a marked air of superiority. "I heard his widow's cousin lived with him at the manor. How fortunate he has an *older* relation available to care for his daughter."

Lucinda gasped, but Althea answered her calmly enough. "Yes, it is, for Lord Keswick has scant patience with misses just out of the schoolroom and lacking in manners."

The barb hit home and Regina's eyes darkened with anger. "We shall see about that, *Miss* Underwood," she said, and turned her back on them.

"Oh, Thea, well done." Lucinda laughed.

"No, it was not. I am a fool to have allowed the chit to put me out of countenance."

"She deserved it nevertheless. Someone needs to teach her some manners. Do not let her disturb you."

But she had disturbed her, and Althea owned it silently. Miss Montague's tall, slender build had made her feel uncomfortably short and awkward beside her. And the girl's air of superiority annoyed her beyond reason. Keswick had openly flirted with her and a vision of Miss Montague as Lady Keswick suddenly assailed Althea. The young woman might become Meredith's stepmother, and as such have much to say about the child's future.

"Althea? My dear, are you ill? You look extremely pale."

"I am fine, Lucy, although I suddenly feel stifled

in here. Lady Penhallow keeps her rooms so warm. I believe I shall just step out on the terrace for a breath of air."

Lucinda moved to accompany her, but Althea waved her back. She needed a few minutes alone to compose herself. There was a small balcony off the drawing room, and she slipped out the French doors unnoticed, just as the gentlemen returned to the room.

Lady Penhallow instructed two footmen to roll back the carpets and sent another one to fetch the musicians she'd hired for the evening. Standing at the far end of the room, she rang a small bell to gain her guests' attention.

"I know our young people will enjoy a few country dances, and the musicians will set up in the far corner of the room," she said, gesturing to where a trio of men were positioning themselves with their instruments. "For those of you who do not care to dance, there are whisk tables in the green room." She motioned to her husband and, engaging his arm, led the older generation from the room just as the musicians began tuning their instruments.

Keswick laughed openly as Regina Montague and Elizabeth Fielding positioned themselves next to him. He agreeably requested Miss Fielding's hand for the first set and Miss Montague's for the next.

George Selwyn looked around the room in search of Althea while the other young men hurried to choose their partners. He noticed that the terrace door was ajar and stepped out onto the dark balcony. It was not very large, just running the length of the doors, and perhaps six feet wide. Althea stood near the edge in the cool air, her eyes fastened on the mountains across Derwent Water, and was so lost in thought that she did not hear him approach.

"Althea? What are you doing out here? You will catch cold standing in this damp air."

Startled, she turned, her arm brushing against his, and was a little off balance. "George! Gracious, you startled me. Have the gentlemen returned then?"

"Yes, just a few moments ago. I was looking for you and noticed the door ajar. How come you to be on the terrace alone?"

"I just stepped out for a moment—it seemed so close in there, but you are right. The wind has picked up and it feels damp now."

George blocked her path. He thought she had never looked more beautiful than in the moonlight. The cool breeze stirred the soft waves of her hair and molded the lines of her gown against her slender body. Involuntarily, he lifted a hand to caress her shoulder. "Althea—"

"Listen! I hear the musicians beginning to play. How kind of Lady Penhallow to provide us with dancing," she said, smiling, and tried to put some enthusiasm into her words. "Do let us join the others. You may have the first dance, George."

There was a pause as the musicians settled themselves, and in the sudden silence Althea heard a distinct click and saw the terrace door shut. She was facing the windows and thought she caught a glimpse of blue silk in front of the door. With a sinking feeling she took a step forward and reached for the doorknob.

"Here, allow me," George said, and stepped in front of her. He rattled the knob and, when he realized it was locked, tapped on the window. It was fruitless. The trio had begun playing, and no one could hear him above the sound of the music. "Of all the—"

"It is no use, George. We shall just have to wait until the dance ends and then try to attract someone's attention."

"My apologies, Althea. I am positive I left the door ajar, but someone must have shut it without realizing we were out here."

"Undoubtedly," she murmured, watching a swirl of blue silk glide across the room. "Well, we shall have to make the best of it and, when we go in, treat it all as a jest."

"Of course, but you must realize people will still talk. Althea, I wish you would reconsider and allow me the right to take care of you. I know I promised not to mention it again, but surely Keswick's return has changed everything."

"Hush, George. This is hardly the place or the time to renew your proposal. Drat. I believe it is starting to rain."

The drops began falling in a gentle patter, but then came down more heavily. They both moved closer to the door, but the wind was from the south and blew the rain in. Althea shivered in her thin gown. George struggled out of his coat and wrapped it about her shoulders. Then he renewed his attack on the door.

The set was a long one and it was a quarter hour before the musicians paused. As luck would have it, Keswick finished the dance near the terrace doors and he heard the furious hammering. He took two long strides and flung the door open.

A gust of wind and rain blew in as George and Althea stepped thankfully through the doors, dripping water on the floor. Someone hurriedly secured the door again, and everyone crowded about them. There were gasps at their sodden condition, a few words of commiseration, and in one or two corners the sounds of sly laughter.

Althea's elaborate coiffure was undone and long, wet strands of hair curled about her face and down her back. She stood there trembling, George's coat, heavy with rain, still wrapped around her shoulders.

"What the devil were you doing out there?" Keswick demanded, his stormy, dark eyes fastened on Althea.

The anger and condemnation in his voice goaded her. Her head came up, and she replied with measured sarcasm, "I stepped out for a breath of air, my lord."

"In the rain? Are you mad?"

"It was not raining earlier," George interrupted quietly. "I went out to find Miss Underwood, and we were just returning when someone closed the door and apparently it locked by accident."

"*Then* it started raining," Althea said with a dagger look at the earl. "Now, if you are quite finished, my lord, I should like to return home at once."

Lucinda appeared beside her, Althea's shawl in her hand. "Come with me, Thea. You cannot go out again in a wet gown. We shall get you dry first." She put a protective arm about her friend and glared at the people surrounding them. The crowd parted reluctantly and let them pass, but the low murmur of voices trailed after them.

"If you do not wish to leave yet, Keswick, I should be glad to drive Miss Underwood home,"

George said and, gesturing to his own clothes, added, "I must leave in any case."

"Thank you, Selwyn, but I brought Miss Underwood here and I will see her home again." The anger underlying the words was sufficient to prevent further argument from George. He merely shrugged and excused himself, but Miss Montague voiced a protest.

"My lord, surely there is no need for you to leave? Send poor Miss Underwood home in your carriage, and my uncle will drive you back to the manor later," she suggested. She laid a hand on his arm and looked up at him, her eyes pleading.

"Thank you, Miss Montague, but as I said, Miss Underwood is my responsibility. It is my duty to see her safely home."

"But you promised to dance with me," she said. Her eyes filled with tears and her mouth turned down in a childish pout.

"There will be other dances," he said coldly. He removed her hand, a flicker of distaste on his face.

Miss Montague caught his expression and quickly sought to make amends. "Forgive me, my lord," she said, lowering her gaze. "Of course you must go. It was most selfish of me to wish to detain you. I fear my disappointment caused me to behave badly. Will you convey to Miss Underwood my regrets? And we will pray she does not fall ill from her soaking."

Lady Penhallow, sailing into the room with Aunt Pysie and Lady Fielding, interrupted. "I have just come from dear Althea, poor girl. She is changing into one of my old gowns and will be ready to leave in a very few moments. I have ordered your carriage brought round, Keswick."

"Thank you, Lady Penhallow. I apologize for the disturbance, and I hope our departure will not spoil your evening."

"It will certainly put a damper on it," she said, and someone laughed aloud at the unintentional pun. She looked around somewhat confusedly. "I cannot imagine how the door came to be locked. It was set ajar deliberately to allow the air to circulate, and even if someone closed it, it should not have been locked."

Lucinda Deerborn, returning to the room to report that Althea was ready to leave, overheard the last. "It is strange, is it not? Almost as though someone locked Althea out deliberately," she remarked, and looked directly at Regina Montague.

Chapter 4

Althea walked into the hall, miserably aware of the picture she must present. She kept her head down, avoiding Cheever's stare, and headed directly for the stairs. Keswick's voice halted her steps.

"I would like a word with you before you retire, Althea."

Aunt Pysie, a pace or two behind Althea, protested. "Surely whatever you feel you must say can wait until morning, Andrew. You can see Althea is chilled and tired. I think she should go to bed at once, and I want Mary to heat some bricks for her. There is nothing more fatal than—"

"I will come up directly, Aunt Pysie," Althea interrupted, and turned to face Keswick. "What is it, *my lord?*"

"We will speak in the library, if you please," he retorted sharply, and turned on his heel without waiting to see if she followed.

Althea considered ignoring him, but Cheever stood impassively by the door. Unless she wished to create a scene, she had little choice. Uncomfortably aware that her borrowed gown was several sizes too large, she pulled her shawl tightly about her shoulders and gathered up a length of the skirt in her hand. She lifted her head and crossed the hall with as much dignity as she could muster.

Keswick stood mutely in front of the desk and stared at her. Unbridled anger coursed through him. She looked like a child dressed for play in her mother's clothes, yet she still had the impudence to defy him. Her huge brown eyes glittered with mockery. The way she lifted her chin and the set of her shoulders in that ridiculous gown challenged him.

"Well, sir, do you intend to keep me standing here all evening?"

"I intend to learn what passed between you and Selwyn on the terrace," he rasped. He'd meant to reason with her, but the words sounded harsh, even to his own ears.

"You were present, I believe, and heard my explanation," Althea said, her voice soft as silk.

"Do not play games with me, Althea. I demand to know what you meant by slipping out onto the balcony with Selwyn."

Her eyes grew luminous and her chin quivered, but she continued to return his look. After a pause she answered in the same soft voice. "I explained how I came to be on the balcony. If you choose not to believe me, there is no more to be said."

"Then you have nothing further to add?"

"Only that you have no right to question me. My affairs are none of your concern."

"I beg to differ with you, my dear. As long as you live in this house, your affairs are very much my concern, and I will not tolerate you meeting my cousin clandestinely."

A blush suffused her face at his implication, and she crossed the room to stand directly before him. "How dare you presume to censure me—or your cousin—when your own name has been bandied the length and breadth of England for the last five years? George is twice the gentleman you could ever hope to be, and I will not stand here and listen to your absurd accusations another moment." She turned abruptly, nearly tripping on the long skirt, and felt Keswick's hand on her arm. Tears threatened to overwhelm her, as they always did when she was angry, but she kept her head down. She would not give him the satisfaction of seeing her cry.

"Althea, listen to me," Keswick ordered. She stood before him, head bent and ready to fly the instant he released her. "Look at me," he demanded, but she refused. He held her easily with one hand and brought his other up beneath her chin, forcing her head up. One teardrop rolled forlornly down her cheek.

His anger evaporated, replaced by a feeling of immense shame. He loosened his grip on her arm and spoke quietly. "Aunt Pysie was right. I should have waited until morning to discuss this with you. Do not cry, little one." With gentle fingers he brushed the tears from her cheeks and then traced the outline of her lips. He looked at her long lashes, wet with tears, and knew an urge to kiss them. Instinctively, he released her arm and slid his hand around her back, drawing her closer.

She stared up at him, unable to move. His eyes seemed to probe the depths of her soul. She knew he was going to kiss her and she was powerless to stop him. Worse, she did not wish to. She felt his warm breath against her cheek and parted her lips slightly. She lifted her head a fraction of an inch and half closed her eyes.

A light knock on the door startled her. Keswick abruptly released her and an instant later Aunt Pysie's gray head peered around the door with a look of inquiry.

"Good heavens, you are still in here! Really, Andrew, I must insist you allow Althea to retire at once. Mary has her bed ready and I prepared a tisane to ward off any fever," she said, stepping into the room.

"I . . . I am coming now, thank you," Althea managed to say, and crossed the room with shaky steps.

"Goodness, child, you look done in. Why, you are as white as a sheet. Here, let me help you."

"No, I shall be fine. I just need to rest," she said, and after hugging the older woman briefly, she fled the room. She half ran across the hall and up the steps, but she could not escape the knowledge that she had wanted Keswick to kiss her.

Althea remained in bed the following day on Aunt Pysie's orders. Although she was neither feverish nor sick, the older woman insisted she needed a full day's rest to recover from her ordeal. Althea was not reluctant to obey. She felt too humiliated to face the numerous people who called. Half the county, or so it seemed, had stopped by Keswick Manor that morning. They claimed concern for her welfare, but Althea knew it was curiosity and a love of gossip that brought them, with only a few exceptions.

She slept fitfully throughout the day and woke late in the afternoon. She stretched, then rang for Mary. Her movement disturbed the kitten, who lay tangled in the sheets. Althea lifted him free and settled him on her lap, allowing him to nibble on her fingers.

"You rang for me, Miss Underwood?" Mary asked a few minutes later. "Did the kitten wake you? I tried to take him downstairs while you was sleeping, but he just kept coming back up here and crying outside your door, so I let him back in."

"No, he is fine, Mary, but I do not believe I can sleep any longer. I would appreciate a cup of tea, however, and you may tell Aunt Pysie I am awake now."

"I'll fetch the tea right away, but Miss Carlyle isn't here. She drove over to the vicar's for tea, and Miss Appletree went with her."

"Oh, did they take Meredith with them then?"

"No, miss. Lady Meredith went off with her papa. Lord Keswick said he was going to Workington and wanted to show her the ocean, and then they was to visit with his friend Lord Sirrus. He told Miss Carlyle not to expect 'em for dinner."

"I see," Althea said, feeling unaccountably depressed at being left alone despite the fact that she did not really wish to see anyone. Coming to a sudden decision, she removed Bows from her lap and swung her legs over the side of the bed. "I shall get dressed, Mary, and come downstairs. Please bring my tea to the blue drawing room and have the fire lit there."

"Yes, miss," the girl agreed, but she seemed hesitant.

"Was there something else, Mary?"

"Miss Carlyle won't like it. She said as how you was to stay in bed and I should bring you tea up here."

Althea smiled. "It will be all right, Mary, I promise you. I shall sit quietly in the drawing room and read until Aunt Pysie returns."

Her maid nodded reluctantly and assisted Althea into a white morning dress of jaconet muslin.

After Mary left, Althea sat at her dressing table and brushed out her hair. It hung well below her shoulders and waved naturally. Normally she twisted it up, but since no one was at home she allowed it to hang down her back and merely drew it away from her face with a ribbon. It will do, she thought, looking into the mirror. She sat still for a moment, studying her reflection.

I wonder if Keswick thinks I'm pretty. The thought flashed into her mind and she blushed at her foolishness. It could not matter in the least what Keswick thought. She admonished herself for being vain and hurried belowstairs. Bows, half asleep on the rug, lifted his head and then leisurely rose and trotted after her.

The day was overcast and chilly, but the drawing room looked inviting with the fire lit and the rose curtains drawn over the windows. Althea had just settled herself on the sofa when Mary entered with the tea tray. Mrs. Pennington bustled in after her.

"I am glad to see you belowstairs, Miss Althea. Miss Carlyle told us how you took a soaking last evening."

"Thank you, Mrs. Pennington, but I am quite recovered now."

"Well, as you didn't come down for lunch, Cook fixed these tiny sandwiches for you. Do try to eat some, Miss Althea. You being such a little thing, you need to keep your strength up."

"I will. They smell delicious."

The room seemed unnaturally quiet after the housekeeper and Mary left. Althea sipped her tea and nibbled on a sandwich, but she had little appetite. She tried to concentrate on her book, but Bows's antics with the braided rug in front of her chair distracted her. The kitten buried his head beneath the rug, backed out, and then attacked it. Amused, Althea scooped him up and placed him beside her on the sofa. She offered him a tidbit from the tray. Bows studied the crust of buttered bread, batted at it with his paw, and then sniffed it.

"What a finicky fellow you are," she said, smiling as he washed the paw that had touched the morsel. Apparently the taste was to his liking and he gobbled down the crust. His tiny nose quivering, he walked across Althea's lap in search of more.

"I see I shall have to teach you some manners," she scolded. She picked the kitten up firmly and returned him to his place on the sofa. "Now sit there like a gentleman and I shall give you another bite."

"Beggin' your pardon, Miss Althea," Mrs. Pennington interrupted. She stood in the door and glanced around the room. "I thought I heard voices in here."

Althea laughed. "You did. Since everyone deserted me, I fear I am reduced to conversing with a kitten."

"Mayhap then you'd be wishful of seeing Mr. Selwyn? I told him as how you were resting, but he asked me to tell you he was here, and he brought you some lovely flowers."

Althea hesitated. She knew she should not receive George alone, especially after the contretemps on the balcony, but she was lonely and a little depressed. Deciding on a compromise, she instructed the housekeeper, "Have Mary come in and settle herself in the corner with some embroidery or something. Then you may show Mr. Selwyn in."

Accordingly, Mary settled in the high-back wing chair, both embarrassed and pleased with her role as chaperone. George was ushered in a few minutes later by Mrs. Pennington and he took the chair opposite Althea. He sat on the edge of the seat, his eyes earnestly searching her face.

Conscious of his regard, Althea busied herself with the mechanics of pouring tea and chattered aimlessly, thanking him for his flowers. George remained silent, and she glanced up to encounter his somber gaze. He looked altogether too serious and she laughed lightly, hoping to ease the tension.

"Gracious, George, do not stare at me so. I am not yet at death's door, I do assure you."

"It is no laughing matter, Althea, though I confess I am vastly relieved to find you so well. I was more than a little alarmed when Lady Fielding told me you were ill and not receiving callers."

"Aunt Pysie insisted I stay in bed today and rest, and I fear I took advantage of it to avoid facing the tattlemongers. Is it not dreadful, George, how people love to gossip?"

"Dreadful, perhaps, but inevitable." He set his cup down carefully on the side table and fixed his eyes on her. "It pains me to say this, but we are the prime topic of conversation today."

"I supposed as much, but do not allow it to worry you. The gossip will pass soon enough. What we need is a good scandal. I wonder if Miss Montague might oblige—she looks ripe for a lark. Or perhaps Lizzie will run off with her captain. I should think that would cast us in the shade."

"You are deliberately making light of this situation, Althea, and I admire you for the brave front you show. What distresses me most, however, is that I should be the one responsible for tarnishing your reputation in the eyes of the county. You cannot know the shockingly vulgar things that are being said, the crude jests and sly innuendos. I realize now there is only one thing we can do."

"George, you are refining too much on this," Althea warned, glancing at Mary. "You must not take the gossips seriously. It does not do, you know, it only encourages more talk."

"I fear you are the one not taking it seriously enough, my dear. Why, it is said we were on the balcony for half an hour, and one young lady even claims to have peered through the window and seen us locked in a passionate embrace."

"How utterly absurd. That sounds like something

66

Lizzie would say—no doubt straight out of one of her novels. Surely no rational person believes we chose to hold a tryst in the middle of a thunderstorm."

"But they do, and I hold myself entirely to blame. He stood, took a step toward the sofa, and dropped to his knees in front of her.

Mary watched with round eyes, uncertain what she should do. A loud cough seemed to have no effect.

George, if he heard the maid, ignored her and took one of Althea's hands in his own. "Althea, my dearest, I ask nothing more than to give you the protection of my name. Do not put me off any longer. You know how much I love you, how much I adore you. Only say you will do me the honor of becoming my wife."

"George, please do not—"

"Althea, you must say yes. I can make you happy," he said, and, rising, slid onto the sofa beside her. He clumsily wrapped his arms around her.

"Mr. Selwyn!" Mary cried, so shocked that she stood up and dropped her needlework.

"George, stop it!" Althea demanded. She struggled to avoid his embrace and the sloppy kisses he rained on her face and shoulders. She managed to shove him backwards and rose at once, her breast heaving.

"You will leave now, if you please, George, or I will have Cheever show you out."

Her voice was cold, and the look of disgust in her eyes caused him to bow his head.

"George? Please do not force me to send for Cheever. I am asking you politely to take your leave."

"You never used to treat me so coldly, Althea."

"You never used to behave so badly, or I would not have received you without your aunt's presence."

"This is Keswick's doing. You have been different since he returned. What is it you want, Althea? The title? Keswick Manor?" He rose, towering over her.

The blind fury in his eyes frightened her. She backed up and was thankful to see Mary dart out the door. Her maid would bring Cheever.

"You'd not be so quick to refuse me if I were the one with the title, would you?"

"I shall try to forget you said that, George," Althea replied. "You are overwrought and cannot mean half of what you are saying."

"I mean it right enough. I understand now what a fool I have been," he ranted, his fists clenched in rage.

The butler appeared in the doorway, and Althea breathed a sigh of relief. "Cheever will show you out now, Mr. Selwyn," she managed to say with a measure of calm.

He glanced briefly at the butler, glared again at Althea, and then strode out of the room without another word. Cheever followed him down the hall.

Althea sank onto the sofa, and Mary hurried to her side. "Cor, miss, I never thought a gentleman would behave like that."

"He was . . . upset, Mary, and we must make allowances. I trust you will not speak of this to anyone."

"Oh, no, miss, I won't, but are you all right? You

68

look a mite out of sorts. Should I pour you some tea?"

"Thank you, Mary, but no. I shall be fine. You run along and I shall just sit here for a bit and read." She picked up her book and looked at the pages through blurred eyes until she heard Mary shut the door. Then she let the tears fall. George had looked at her with such . . . such hatred. She shivered uncontrollably.

In the week that followed, Althea did her best to put the incident with George from her mind. It was not easy, since she held herself equally to blame. She should have made it clear to him that she would never accept his proposal. Instead she'd gently turned aside his previous offers and allowed him to believe she might change her mind. She also knew she'd been wrong to receive him without Aunt Pysie. Just recalling the scene in the drawing room brought blushes to her cheeks and a feeling of revulsion for the sloppy, wet kisses George had managed to land on her face.

The gossip had been easier to ignore. As she'd predicted, it soon passed, and for that she had Keswick to thank. The community was now rife with speculation over the earl's intentions. On Monday he had called on the Hardings and chatted at length with Miss Montague. On Tuesday he had taken the young lady driving. The gossips had been ready to declare it a match, but on Wednesday Keswick had confounded them and called on Elizabeth Fielding. Lizzie had no chance to gloat, however. The earl was seen driving little Sarah Aubrey in his phaeton on Friday. The rumors flew.

Richard Kingsly added fuel to the fire and swaggered about town swearing he intended to teach the earl a lesson. It was noted, however, that he was careful never to confront Keswick directly. Most of his elders wrote him off as a foolish young man overly prone to theatrics.

Althea refused to either listen to or take part in any discussion concerning Keswick and his matrimonial intentions. Lucinda Deerborn, who drove over for tea Sunday afternoon, threw up her hands in disgust.

"It is all very well to sit there and say it is no concern of yours, Thea, but what will you do when he brings one of those chits back here as Lady Keswick? She will be Meredith's stepmother, you know."

"I shall worry about it if and when the event occurs," Althea replied calmly. "Now may we please put an end to this conversation? Tell me instead what you plan to wear to Lady Fielding's on Saturday."

"Nothing new. Papa absolutely refuses to buy me a new gown before next quarter. Mattie is trying to refurbish one of my old ones, and I suppose that will have to do. It is so vexing. Captain Hewlitt is home, and Lizzie told me he brought two of his London friends down with him."

"Then what are you worried about, goose? They can never have seen any of your gowns before."

"How true," Lucy owned, much struck. "But what of you, Thea? Have you decided what to wear?"

"I doubt it matters much. It is hardly likely anyone I would wish to impress will be there."

"Now, Thea, do not speak as though you were

past your prayers. Who knows what Captain Hewlitt's friends will be like? And George will be there, of course."

Althea nodded and hid the uneasiness she felt at facing George again. He had sent her a large bouquet of flowers with a note begging her forgiveness and a plea that they at least remain friends. She was willing enough to forgive him, though his conduct had truly shocked her. What she could not forgive, or easily forget, was the flame of hatred she'd seen in his eyes.

"Keswick will be in attendance, will he not?" Lucy was asking as she pulled on her gloves.

"You would do better to ask Lizzie or Miss Montague. I have no idea, for we have scarcely seen him this last week. He has been too busy making the acquaintance of every young lady in the neighborhood."

"Has he shown a preference for any lady in particular?"

"Only one," Althea replied with a smile.

"Oh, tell me, Thea. I pray it is not Regina Montague or Lizzie Fielding, for it would be beyond bearing. Tell me at once, you wretched girl, who is it?"

Althea laughed. "As far as I know, if any young lady holds an attraction for him, it is Lady Meredith."

"His daughter? Oh, Thea, you beast to tease me so!"

"I am quite serious. Keswick rides with Meredith almost every morning, and he takes her with him to visit the tenants. It will be wonderful if she is not spoiled by all the attention."

Miss Deerborn took her leave, shaking her head

over the inexplicable Lord Keswick. Althea watched her depart without regret. She, too, was puzzled by the earl, but she did not wish to discuss her feelings with anyone. She had avoided Keswick whenever possible, even forgoing her morning rides with Meredith. He, however, did not appear to notice and Meredith did not seem to mind. Althea, accustomed to ranking first in the child's affections, now found herself relegated to second place.

"Is there any tea left?" Keswick asked from the doorway, and Althea jumped. It was as though she had conjured him up.

Meredith entered with him and ran across the room. "Aunt Thea, Tommy has a broken leg. I saw it, and he cannot walk. He fell off his horse, Aunt Thea, and the horse rolled over on top of him and broke his leg."

Althea returned her hug and shot a questioning look over the child's head to Keswick.

"Beresford's youngest boy," he explained, referring to one of the tenants. "Mason told me the boy had taken a bad fall, and we drove over to see for ourselves," he said, stretching out in the chair Lucinda had vacated.

"He has to stay in bed, Aunt Thea, and it will be a long time before he can ride again. I do not fall off my pony, do I, Papa?"

"No, princess, and I hope you will not rush your fences either, which is what Tommy did. More bottom than sense."

Althea handed him his tea and then fixed a cup of half milk, half tea for Meredith. She looked up to find Keswick regarding her curiously.

"Mrs. Beresford inquired after you. She said she

hoped her boys did not offend you the last time you visited."

"Whatever gave her that idea? They are good boys, all of them. Even Sammy," she said, and smiled suddenly. "The last time we visited, he dressed a pig up in one of Mrs. Beresford's old hats and pretended it was Lady Penhallow come to tea."

"So I heard. Mrs. Beresford apparently fears you might not have found the incident amusing. She said she'd not seen much of you of late, not since I returned home, in fact."

"We used to visit the tenants every week, Papa. Aunt Thea said it was our duty," Meredith told him, and hungrily eyed the chocolate cake.

Althea deftly transferred a slice to a plate and handed it to Meredith with a napkin.

"It seems to be a duty she has forgotten," Keswick drawled, his keen eyes intent on Althea.

"Not forgotten, sir, merely abdicated. It is not my place to visit the tenants now."

"I told you I did not wish to make any changes here. The tenants miss you, Althea. I have been charged with numerous messages for you."

"Whether or not you wish to do so, your return *does* change things. The tenants will adjust soon enough."

"I doubt that. These people consider you their friend, and they are anxious to know why you have not ridden out. They will not take kindly to me if my return means you will no longer visit. Come now, Althea, you cannot wish me to be on the outs with my tenants. Say you will come with Merry and me tomorrow. We plan to visit the Braithwrites and the Edwards."

"Mrs. Braithwrite makes her own wine, doesn't she, Aunt Thea?"

"Yes, darling, and always insists I have a glass. That is one pleasure I could easily forgo."

"I shall drink the wine, if you will come," Keswick promised recklessly.

"Please, Aunt Thea. I miss riding with you," Meredith pleaded, her eyes full of appeal.

"Oh, very well, but I shall hold you to your promise, Keswick, and I warn you—it is dandelion wine."

Meredith did not understand what the adults found amusing, but she was pleased all the same. She wanted to stretch out the day and keep both Althea and her father there with her. "Papa, tell Aunt Thea about the strange gentleman we saw."

The laughter died out of his eyes, and Althea looked an inquiry.

"We chanced upon Lord Filmore near the crossroads."

"Oh. I did not know he was back."

"No, nor I. Apparently he has just returned."

"Surely it is a coincidence? Did he speak to you?"

Keswick nodded, recalling the unpleasant encounter. "He said he was pleased to hear I had returned and that he always knew our paths would cross again someday."

"The man was dressed all in black, Aunt Thea, and rode a black horse like Papa's."

"He still wears mourning then?" Althea asked sadly.

Keswick nodded and changed the subject, but Althea could not so easily forget it. Shortly before Keswick had gone abroad, he had engaged in a card game with Jack Filmore's older brother, Oli-

74

ver. Lord Filmore had been in his cups. He had lost several hands to the earl but refused to quit the game. By the end of the evening, he'd staked his entire fortune and lost.

Althea had been visiting her cousin at the time. She readily recalled the sight of Oliver Filmore when he stumbled from the house, a broken man. Keswick, to his credit, had immediately sent all the vowels he'd won back to Filmore with a footman. He'd told her that he could not take advantage of a man as inebriated as Filmore had been, but Oliver had never learned of his generosity. He had drowned himself in Derwent Water the same evening.

Chapter 5

Althea rose the following morning with second thoughts about the wisdom of spending the day in Lord Keswick's company. She half hoped it would rain, providing her with a reasonable excuse for staying home, but her luck was out. The sun crested against a clear blue sky, promising a golden day to tempt the most jaded of persons. Althea was not immune to its promise. She drew open the window and leaned out, luxuriating in the warmth of the sun on her skin. It evaporated her doubts as easily as it dried the dew on the grass. This was clearly not a day to waste inside.

Althea dressed and hurried belowstairs. She heard Keswick's deep-throated chuckle and Meredith's gleeful giggles even before she reached the hall. Their merriment was contagious and she paused in the door of the breakfast room, smiling. Keswick sprawled easily in his chair and appeared more at ease and content than Althea could ever recall seeing him. His dark hair was ruffled and his crisp white shirt was open at the collar, but it was not just the informality of his attire. There was an unguarded look in his eyes, and his smile for once held no trace of sarcasm.

Meredith suddenly reached up and tweaked his

nose. Keswick grabbed her in a fierce hug and nibbled at her neck until her screams of delight echoed through the room.

Althea shook her head in mock disapproval as she entered and took her place at the table. "The pair of you deserve to be relegated to the nursery."

"Papa's a bear, Aunt Thea," Meredith explained, leaning against his broad chest.

"So I see," she replied, surveying the scraps remaining on the table. "Did you save me any breakfast?"

Meredith giggled and Keswick grinned at her unabashed, but there was a warm look in his dark eyes that clearly conveyed his approval. Althea returned his smile and suddenly realized she was looking forward to their ride.

Meredith begged her to hurry and it was not long before the trio headed for the stables. Althea and Keswick strolled together, but Meredith pranced ahead, stopping every two feet to urge them on. Althea thought the child looked charming in a blue riding habit especially designed for her by a local seamstress. The divided skirt allowed her to ride astride instead of sidesaddle as was the custom for ladies. It was a miniature of Althea's own habit, and she suddenly wondered if Keswick would take her to task for allowing it, as Selwyn often did. Thus far he'd said nothing, but a woman who rode astride placed herself slightly beyond the pale. Althea was ready to defend herself and Meredith, but the earl, beyond commenting that both his ladies looked lovely, did not mention their attire.

Keswick's black stallion and Meredith's pony were saddled and waiting just outside the stables, but Mason was obviously surprised to see Althea dressed for riding. He quickly ordered a groom to ready Miss Underwood's mare and apologized for the delay.

"It's quite all right, Mason. I should have sent word I would be riding this morning. Was that a new groom?"

"Yes, miss. Danny gave his notice a few days back. Said he got a better offer and this boy happened to turn up looking for a place, so I thought I'd give him a try. Seems to know horses right enough."

She agreed, noting the lad's capable manner when he brought out her mare. The boy was tall and thin, with the sort of dark complexion that comes from hours spent in the sun. He handled her mare easily, and she suspected a wiry strength lay beneath his skinny arms. He seemed respectful enough, kept his head down, and only nodded shyly when she spoke to him.

Keswick gave her a leg up, and a few moments later they cantered toward the lane. Althea breathed deeply of the morning air and looked up at the mountains. "Say what you will about our climate, but you must own the summer is spectacular."

"Easily," Keswick agreed. "It's the other ten months of the year one must live through that gives people pause. Our county is undoubtedly the wettest in all England, but I love it just the same."

"What, more than Paris or Rome? You spent so much time abroad we thought you would become an expatriate."

"No danger of that," he replied lightly, but she thought he seemed sad, or perhaps regretful, as he scanned the surrounding landscape.

"Why *did* you stay away so long? We expected when . . . when Deborah died, you would come home at once."

"Lord knows I wanted to," he said, his gaze still on the mountains. After a moment he glanced at her. "I went abroad because I knew it would be easier on Deborah. It seemed I threw her into a fit of terror if I so much as walked into a room where she was sitting, and I did not want to upset her while she was . . . with child. I never could understand what it was about me that frightened her. I swear I never gave her cause."

There was real regret as well as bitterness in his voice, and Althea could see that Deborah's unreasonable fear of him had given him pain. She almost felt sorry for him.

"I think it was partly because you're so *large,*" she finally told him with a rare smile of sympathy. "It made Deb nervous. And when she got nervous, you responded by becoming angry, which made her even more nervous. You do look quite ominous when you are angry, you know, and Deborah led such a sheltered life. She was sick a great deal, and was very compliant when she was well, so I do not believe anyone ever spoke harshly to her. You, sir, with your loud ways and raging good health, were quite a shock."

"I suppose, but *you* were never afraid of me. I believe you once referred to me as a beetle-headed bedlamite incapable of—"

"Keswick! I could not have behaved so rudely," she interrupted, laughing.

"Ah, but you did, and on more than one occasion. Of course, I will concede you were frequently provoked, and more often than not, when you raked me down, it was in defense of your cousin."

Althea sobered abruptly. "We will not discuss that, if you please. What is past is past, and better left there. We could go on for years blaming ourselves and rehashing events, but it would not bring Deborah back, so it is rather senseless, do you not agree?"

"I do except . . . I hate to think you still hold me to blame."

Althea knew not how to answer him and looked away from his probing eyes. An uncomfortable silence grew between them and then she heard Keswick sigh.

"It was an unfortunate marriage, Althea, but at least grant me credit for clearing out when Deborah made it obvious she could not bear my presence."

"You did indeed, and stayed away long after it was necessary. Why did you not return after Deborah died, Keswick? It is something I have always wondered about."

"What was there to come home for? I knew Kingsly would be ripe to call me out on some pretext or other, and after that business with Filmore—cowardly of me, I suppose—I could not bear to face everyone." He paused for a moment before adding, "Especially you. I feared you might hate me."

Althea glanced away. Making an effort to keep her voice light, she replied, "Perhaps, then, it was a good thing you remained abroad for so long. I think I did hate you, at least at first."

"And now?"

The question hung on the morning air.

"Papa, Aunt Thea, come on," Meredith called, impatient with their slow pace. A low fence lay across the meadow just ahead. She wanted to jump it and surprise Althea. She'd practiced it for two weeks under her father's eye.

"Right you are, princess. Lead the way," Keswick called, and lightly spurred his black.

Althea knew the fence lay ahead; she'd ridden this way so many times with Meredith. She expected the girl to check her pony, dismount, and open the gate. But Meredith did not check. She rode straight at the fence with Keswick keeping pace a few yards behind her.

Althea watched breathlessly. If she called out, she stood the risk of startling Meredith, but the urge to do so was strong. She pulled her bay up short. Her knees gripped the mare, and her hands held the reins tightly, ready to fly to the child's aid if need be.

The pony lifted off his hind legs, rising easily in the air. Meredith leaned forward above his neck, pushing up slightly out of the saddle, her tiny back perfectly straight. They soared over the fence in one fluid motion. Althea breathed a sigh of relief. She watched Meredith gallop her pony a short distance, slow, and then turn to wave triumphantly.

"Did you see, Aunt Thea? Did you see me jump?"

"I saw you," she called, "and if you ever dare frighten me like that again, I shall beat you!"

Keswick laughed aloud, but not unkindly, and brought his stallion alongside Althea. "She was in no danger, I promise you."

"You might have warned me."

"And spoiled her surprise? I could not be so unkind. You are not truly angry, are you?"

"No," she replied, reluctantly smiling at his look of boyish appeal.

"Good, then let us show Merry she's not the only one who can jump." He gave the black his head, racing for the fence. Althea spurred her mare and was only a pace behind him.

It should have been an easy jump, but unbelievably she saw Keswick falling to the side and swerved her own horse to the left. She brought her surefooted mare down lightly even as she heard Meredith scream and saw the black galloping off riderless. Althea glanced back and saw Keswick sitting by the fence. Relieved he appeared unhurt, she sped after his stallion. She didn't have to chase him far. A whistle from Keswick curbed the horse's headlong flight, and Althea brought her bay alongside him. Speaking softly, afraid of startling the black, she leaned forward and grabbed the reins.

A moment later she dismounted and walked both horses back to the gate. Keswick was still on the ground, leaning back against the fence, with Meredith crouching beside him. He gave Althea a lopsided grin.

"I suppose I shall never hear the end of this. It should be a lesson to Merry not to become complacent, even with an easy jump. I should have paid more attention to what I was about."

"Did you break your leg, did you, Papa?" Meredith asked, tears in her eyes. "Tommy broke his leg when he fell."

"No, princess, so dry your eyes. However, I believe I might have sprained my ankle. It hurts like the devil. Would you be a good girl and ride back to the stables? Tell Mason what happened and have him bring a carriage."

Althea, about to object, was silenced by a warning glance from Keswick. She said nothing as Meredith kissed him.

"I will, Papa, and I'll ride fast, too."

Althea gave the child a leg up, cautioned her to be careful, and watched as she cantered down the lane. It was still early morning and they were not far from the house, so it was unlikely Meredith would come to any harm. Still, she disliked sending her off alone. Keswick had best have a good reason, she thought, turning to question him.

The pain she saw reflected in his eyes chased all other thoughts from her mind and brought her instantly to his side. With a measure of concern she knelt beside him. "Are you badly hurt, Keswick?"

He shook his head. "I wished a word with you in private. I felt the saddle slipping the instant I took the jump. I thought the girth had not been properly buckled."

"I cannot believe Mason could be so careless!"

"This was not carelessness. The strap was cut through," he said, gesturing to the saddle lying beside him. "I had a look at it while you were fetching Mercury. It was bound to give the instant I put my full weight on it."

"Cut?" Althea drew back, appalled. "But . . . but that would mean it was deliberate. Who would do such a thing?"

"Good question, my dear."

"But if what you say is true, you could have broken your neck."

"No doubt that was someone's intent," he replied with a wry grin, his eyes seeming to mock her. "Would you have cared, Thea?" The words were spoken in jest, but he watched her closely.

"Certainly. I would not like to see *anyone* injured in such a manner." She rose, a blush betraying her inner turmoil, and busied herself checking the black's legs. "Mercury does not seem to have suffered any," she called. To all appearances she was concerned only with the black stallion, but her mind dwelt on the way Keswick had looked at her. He'd called her Thea, too, just as he had that night five years ago. The night before he'd left.

Althea left their horses to the groom's care and rode home in the carriage with Keswick. Although he had insisted he was not in much pain, he leaned tiredly against the seat with his eyes shut. Althea observed him closely. He never uttered a word of protest, but his lips curled into a grimace when the carriage jolted against a rut in the road and she noticed the way his hands were curled into fists. She thought he would be more comfortable with his boot off, but Keswick stubbornly refused any assistance until they arrived home.

By resting most of his weight against Mason, the earl was able to limp into the south drawing room on the first floor. The room, which was rarely used except for formal occasions, had the advantage of housing an exceptionally long sofa. Keswick was eased down upon it, his face drawn and white. Althea went at once to fetch him a glass of brandy, for he looked close to passing out, and she nearly bumped into Meredith. The child stood clinging to the door, her eyes round and dark in her pale face. Scared to death, Althea thought, and stopped long enough to hug her. "Your papa will be fine, sweetheart. Run and find Miss Appletree for me."

Meredith stood where she was, her tiny face

screwed up into the same stubborn lines as her father's. Althea sighed. She'd have to do something about Meredith, but at the moment her first concern was Keswick. She hurried back and found Aunt Pysie beside the sofa, fussing over him.

"Dr. Mayhew has been sent for, but I do not believe we should wait any longer to remove that boot, Andrew, and I do not like the look of your color."

Althea silently agreed, but she gently moved the older woman aside and handed Keswick the brandy. She received a ghost of a smile in return and watched him drain the glass.

"Send for Evans. He will know what to do," Keswick told her, sounding somewhat better for the brandy.

Aunt Pysie moved closer to adjust a cushion and accidentally knocked against his leg. At Keswick's roar of pain, she hastened to apologize, half-near tears.

Althea hurriedly put an arm about the older woman and spoke to her in a whisper. "Aunt Pysie, when they remove his boot, Keswick will no doubt be in a great deal of pain and may not realize what he is saying. Meredith is already frightened and I do not think she should be in here. Would you—"

"Of course, my dear, of course. Do not say another word. You are absolutely right." She patted Althea's hand and then bustled across the room. "Meredith, darling, come with me. We must tell Miss Appletree what has occurred, and then after you change you may help me prepare a restorative for your papa."

Althea watched them leave before turning back to Keswick. He looked his gratitude and stretched out a hand to her. Without thinking, she moved closer to the sofa and took his hand in her own. The warmth and strength of his fingers was strangely comforting, and she was inexplicably grateful for his touch. Bewildered, she stared down at him, her brown eyes a mirror of her confusion.

"Do not fret, Thea," he advised gently, making an effort to smile. "Miss Appletree will reassure Merry, and old Mayhew will soon have my foot in order."

"I am more concerned with whom—"

"We will talk about that later," Keswick broke in, releasing her hand. He motioned toward the door, where Cheever and Mason stood talking.

She nodded her understanding, but there was no time to say more in any event. Mason thought he heard the doctor's carriage and scurried down the hall, with the butler moving ponderously in his wake. Keswick's valet appeared in the door and surveyed the room with an air of unshakable calm. Evans was easily as tall as the earl, but only half his weight, yet he never hesitated to dictate to his master.

"Evans, old man, I am glad you are here. See if you can get this boot off before Mayhew gets his rough hands on me."

His man stood beside him and moved his hands gently down the calf of the earl's leg. "I am afraid, sir, the foot is too swollen. We shall have to cut your boot free."

"Then do it, man."

Evans sighed, looking with regret at the boots. "A pity you wore the Wellingtons. If you will just wait one moment, sir, I shall fetch a knife."

"Blasted man cares more for my boots than my foot," Keswick muttered.

"I doubt that," Althea said, smoothing his hair back from his brow. Was it only her imagination, she wondered, or did he feel feverish?

She was thankful when Evans returned so quickly, but one glance at the wicked-looking knife he wielded turned her queasy. She held tight to Keswick's hand and stared at the painting of a hunt on the far wall while the valet sliced through the boot. The swishing sound of the leather being cut apart grated on her nerves.

She heard Keswick groan, and when she dared look again, Evans was handing him the brandy. His foot lay exposed, discolored and badly swollen. Althea felt faint and was thankful when Evans put out a hand to steady her.

"I should not worry, Miss Underwood. His lordship has been through much worse. I have no doubt he will be himself within a few days. Not like him to take a toss, though. Did something startle that stallion of his?"

She hesitated, aware that Keswick did not wish anyone else to know of his suspicions. Fortunately, the timely appearance of the butler saved her from answering.

Cheever begged pardon for disturbing her and quietly informed her that Mr. Selwyn had called. "I did not quite like to show him in here, miss, and put him in the blue room instead. However, I did take the liberty of telling the gentleman that you were otherwise engaged."

"Thank you, Cheever. I dislike leaving his lordship—"

"Go on, Althea," Keswick said, releasing her

hand. "I would prefer that you see my cousin, and if he should inquire, pray tell him I am in perfect health." The sardonic glint in his eyes made her uneasy.

"Surely, my lord, you cannot believe your own cousin would—"

"Would gossip? Indeed I do, and I would as lief not have it spread about that I took a toss over a fence a child could jump. Be a good girl and spare me that embarrassment."

Cheever stood immobile while Althea looked from him to Keswick, clearly undecided.

"The gentleman was most insistent, miss, otherwise I would not have admitted him," the butler pointed out in a helpful manner.

"Very well. Please tell Mr. Selwyn I shall see him directly and, Cheever, ask Aunt Pysie to join us."

Althea arrived at the door of the drawing room a quarter hour later and observed George nervously pacing near the windows. She watched him for a moment before making her presence known.

"Cheever said you insisted on seeing me, Mr. Selwyn; however, I can only spare you a moment or two."

George spun about at the sound of her voice and crossed the room with his hands outstretched as though he intended to take hers. After one glance at her countenance, he dropped his arms to his sides.

"Althea, it is most kind of you to see me. I know I deserve to be barred at the door."

He sounded so desperately contrite, she felt a pang of sympathy for him. She relented her stern manner sufficiently to take a seat on the sofa and gestured for him to sit opposite.

"This is a small community, Mr. Selwyn, and should it be observed that we cannot be civil to each other, it would occasion a great deal of unpleasant talk."

"It would, indeed, and it was that thought that gave me hope you might agree to see me."

"I will see you, sir, when and as I must, although under the circumstances I would much prefer that you no longer call here."

"I deserve that and do not blame you. I came solely to offer you my apologies, Althea. I have been tortured this past week, unable to eat or sleep properly for remembering . . . I was dreadfully out of line and said such shameful things, I wonder you speak to me at all. My only excuse is that I was overcome with disappointment at your refusal."

His blue eyes beseeched her, putting her much in mind of the beggars she'd once seen in London. Embarrassed, Althea glanced away, nervously pleating the skirt of her riding habit. She hoped Aunt Pysie would come in soon.

"Please, Althea, allow me—"

"I think it would be best if we did not discuss this further," she said curtly, lifting her hand. "Your conduct was such that I can no longer be comfortable in your company."

"I know, and it pains me to see you draw away so. Althea, grant me a second chance. I swear I shall never again press my attentions on you—but cry friends with me. I know now I can hope for nothing more, but your friendship would mean a great deal. I cannot bear to lose that as well."

He spoke eloquently, his eyes never leaving her face. She glanced up at him then, only for a brief second or two, but long enough for him to see her weakness and he quickly pressed his advantage.

"Can you truly forget all the years we have been friends? The rides we have shared, the picnics? The times when I have helped you with your problems and provided you with the companionship you needed? Althea, do not throw it all away because I acted insanely for one moment. Can you not balance that against all the rest and find it in yourself to forgive me? I swear you will never regret it."

Her heart was not proof against such an entreaty, and mindful that she, too, was partly to blame, she relented slightly. "I should like to forgive you, Mr. Selwyn, but your opinion of me was such—"

"No! Do not shame me more by repeating those infamous words. My opinion of you is as high as ever. I spoke rashly, driven by despair. I could never think ill of you, and I beg you to forget I ever spoke so."

She studied his hopeful face for a long moment before suddenly smiling and holding out her hand. "You win, George. You may consider us friends, but let us agree never to speak of this matter again."

"Done," he said, and took her hand in his, but mindful of his promise, he released her quickly. "I know we are indeed friends when you call me George in just such a manner. I cannot tell you how pleased I am, dear Althea. I only hope the others will not censure you for such a generous gesture."

"The others?"

"Did you not tell Aunt Pysie and Keswick what occurred? Oh, do not think I reproach you, Althea! You had every reason to be agitated, and it would only be natural if you had confided in Aunt Pysie."

"You may put your mind at ease, George. No one is aware of what occurred other than my maid, who, I assure you, is most discreet."

Before he could reply, Aunt Pysie waddled in. She greeted him warmly enough to assure him that Althea had spoken the truth, offered him her cheek to kiss, and inquired mildly where he had been for the past week. The talk turned general, and if Althea was impatient for him to go, she did not show it. They spoke comfortably together as old friends will, and there was only one bad moment when George asked about Keswick.

"He has been extremely busy about the estate," Althea said quickly. "But I will be sure to tell him that you asked after him."

Aunt Pysie looked at her strangely, but George noticed nothing amiss and rose to take his leave.

"I shall look forward to seeing you both at Lady Fielding's on Saturday, then?"

Althea nodded, then walked with him to the door. "I believe everyone in the county will be there, even Captain Hewlett. I hear he is home and has brought a couple of fine London gentlemen up with him, so it should be a grand turn-out."

"And my cousin? Will he escort you?"

"I would not dare speak for Keswick," Althea said with a laugh. "Certainly he *should* attend, but he does not much heed the conventions."

"Well, if you should need an escort, you know I would be honored to oblige."

"Thank you, George, but even if Keswick absents himself, Aunt Pysie and I can manage."

Aunt Pysie was waiting for her in the hall and laid a hand on Althea's arm. "That was quick thinking, my dear. I nearly blurted out how Andrew hurt his ankle, and he would have been furious with me had I told George. Not that I think George would have twitted him about it, but then gentlemen take such strange notions into their heads."

"How very true, Aunt. Keswick is embarrassed and would dislike it excessively if everyone knew he took a toss over such a low jump."

"Careless of him, but there, we all have our off days, do we not? I am sure it could happen to anyone . . . although I cannot ever recollect Andrew being unseated, not even when he was a boy and such a bruising rider. He and George were always getting up races and jumping everything in sight. I feared one or the other would break his neck, but the only thing they ever damaged was their own pride. Is it not odd how gentlemen place so much stock on being superb horsemen? I daresay it would be best to give out that Andrew has injured his ankle and not mention how."

Althea nodded, but her mind was on other things. "Do you know if Dr. Mayhew arrived?"

"Oh, did I not mention it? He was with Andrew when I joined you. I had a word with Evans, poor man. Andrew is already restless, and Evans said it will be a job keeping him off his feet for three days, which is likely what the doctor will recommend."

"I shall see if I can help," Althea promised, and walked down the hall to the south drawing room. Mason nodded to her as he left, and she entered in time to stop an argument between Keswick and his valet.

Evans turned to her thankfully. "Miss Underwood, perhaps your word will carry some weight with his lordship. He insists on rising, though the

92

doctor just told him he must rest his ankle for at least three days."

"These doctors are all alike and only want to coddle a person. I can manage perfectly well if you will just give me a cane. I have had worse breaks than this and never stayed abed."

"Not in your feet, my lord. It is not like when you broke your arm or got pinked in the shoulder fighting that duel in Paris."

"A duel? Now that is something I should like to hear about," Althea said, moving a chair nearer to the sofa. "Evans, would you ask Mrs. Pennington to bring us some tea?"

The valet nodded and hurried from the room before Keswick could protest. He glared at her instead. "Stay if you like, Thea, but I will not discuss a duel with you or with any other female."

"Oh, do try not to be so stuffy, Keswick. What harm can it do? Evans said you were pinked—does that mean you lost?"

"Certainly not. And it was the merest scratch."

"Oh. I rather thought a duel was over when first blood was drawn. Did you fight to the death then?"

"No! Althea, I told you I'd not discuss this. A duel is hardly a fit topic for a young lady's ears."

"I see. It was *over* a young lady. Did you care for her a great deal? Was she very pretty, Keswick?"

"Yes, although not as pretty as you, and without a thought in her head. Now, will you give it up? If you wish to be useful, pull that chessboard over here. Do you still play?"

He sounded aggravated, but at least he was smiling, and she positioned the board between them. When Mrs. Pennington brought in the tea, she found them happily battling over Althea's queen.

"That was a dastardly trick, my lord, and I promise you shall pay for it," Althea threatened.

"No, no, it was your own doing. You should never trust the bishop, my dear. Now, then, I have captured your queen, so you might as well surrender. You are completely defenseless."

Althea looked up at him, her brown eyes brimming with laughter. "Am I?" Then she moved her knight a block over and forward two.

"Check and checkmate, my lord."

"I'll be dammed," Keswick muttered after a moment. "Did your uncle teach you that maneuver?" He adjusted his cushion so that he could study the board.

She poured tea for them both while he considered his choices. A puny pawn blocked him on the left. If he moved to the right, he'd be in line with her castle. Checkmated either way.

Keswick glanced up and caught her impudent grin. He smiled, too, but could not refrain from teasing her. "Perhaps we should continue this game later."

"Continue, sir? I thought the game over, but I shall allow your diversion if you will tell me what you are thinking." Her hand lightly brushed his as she handed him a cup.

"Ah, well. I am thinking it's a dashed inconvenient time to be handicapped by my ankle. And I am thinking you look very fetching in that riding habit. I meant to ask before, did you have it especially cut for you?"

"Yes. Now be serious, Keswick. Do you really suspect George had some hand in causing your accident? Is that why you did not want him to know you took a fall?"

94

"I cannot believe my own cousin would try to do me in, not even for the sake of the estate and title. George and I might not always rub together well, but he knows I would not hesitate to help him, if he needed me, and I'd like to think the same was true of him. I just did not wish word to get around."

"Around to whom? Come now, obviously you suspect someone."

"Well, it strikes me as the sort of backhanded thing Kingsly might try. For all his bravado, he'd never meet me face-to-face. And then there is Filmore."

"Jack Filmore? No, I cannot believe it of him. You were such close friends once. He could never harm you."

"I fear he hates me now and could very well do so. But there are a score of others to choose from. It seems I have unwittingly offended any number of people and never realized it." The words were lightly said, but Keswick stared at his ankle, his dark eyes brooding.

"Perhaps even the man you fought the duel with," Althea teased, trying to brighten his mood.

"A pleasant thought, but I am afraid the person who did this is someone I know here. Someone who knows my habits and the people in the neighborhood."

"I will not believe that! We cannot even be sure there was an attempt on your life. After all, we have no proof the strap was deliberately cut. Perhaps it was extremely worn and the new groom did not notice."

"Did you happen to see Mason leaving when you came in?"

"Yes, of course. Why?" she asked, wondering at

the abrupt change of topic and the sardonic look in Keswick's eyes.

"He came to tell me the new groom disappeared shortly after we rode out this morning."

Chapter 6

The groom's disappearance cast a sinister light on Keswick's accident, and it was much on Althea's mind. She questioned Mason the following morning, but he could tell her no more than he had told the earl. The new lad had turned up the same afternoon Danny had quit. Mason had been inclined to think it a coincidence until the boy disappeared. The lad had said his name was Grimsby, but if Mason's suspicions were correct, it meant nothing. Unlikely the boy gave his real name if he was up to devilment, and it looked that way now, Mason had said. All he could tell her was that the lad didn't come from Cumberland or anywhere nearby.

Althea agreed and dismissed thoughts of finding Grimsby. She asked Mason to keep an ear open for news of Danny, thinking someone on the estate might know where he'd gone. She was convinced he'd been lured away deliberately, and if they could only find him, they might be able to learn who was behind this business.

She could not be easy until they learned the truth. Her head pounding and nearly exhausted from several sleepless nights, she went tiredly back to the house. Determined to discuss the matter with Keswick, she headed for the drawing room, hoping to find him alone. Althea glanced through the door and saw Meredith sitting in the curve of his arm. Buttons lay at the bottom of the sofa, beneath Keswick's bandaged foot. She watched the pair, their heads bent close together, black curls mingling. It was a tender, loving scene, father and daughter united and content with each other. A surge of anger, of irrational jealousy, shot through Althea.

"Meredith! Remove your puppy at once, and you will please remember to sit in a chair like a proper young lady."

The two dark-haired ones gazed up at her in surprise.

Althea realized she'd spoken more sharply than she intended, and she softened her voice. "Buttons could jar your papa's foot and cause him a great deal of pain. You would not wish that, would you?"

"No, Aunt Thea." Meredith obediently picked up her puppy and placed him at her feet as she slid into a large armchair. She sat quietly, eyes down and hands folded neatly in her lap.

Althea turned to Keswick, who grinned at her broadly. Imagining his dark eyes mocked her, she turned her anger in his direction. "As for you, my lord, I can see you are feeling more the thing, but you should not allow Meredith to bother you."

"I never allow anyone to bother me, Thea, as you well know. Are you not rather militant this morning?"

"I cannot see where your accident is cause for jesting, sir," she retorted. "I have just come from seeing Mason and—"

"You will oblige me by not inquiring further into this," he interrupted, all trace of humor gone. "I told you I would attend to the matter. If you wish to be helpful, I suggest you take Meredith and visit the Braithwrites. They are expecting us and I should not like to disappoint them."

"No, Papa! I want to stay here with you," Meredith cried.

"I thought you liked riding with me, Meredith," Althea said lightly, though she was hurt by the child's words.

"I do, Aunt Thea, only Papa is sick, and I want to stay here with him."

"You run along with your aunt, princess. It is our obligation to visit the tenants, and since I cannot go, you will have to act as my deputy. I shall be here when you get back, you know, and you may tell me all about your visit."

She nodded, but was clearly disappointed. Althea sent her off to change into her riding habit, then waited till the child had left the room before confronting Keswick.

"I take leave to remind you, my lord, that I am not your groom or your valet to be ordered about as you please. The attack on you concerns us all, and the sooner we learn who was behind it, the sooner—"

"I hate to keep interrupting you, my dear, but you appear not to have heard me. I said I will attend to the matter and I will thank you to accept my word. This has all the earmarks of a boy acting out of pique and I suspect Kingsly. However, if it should prove more serious, I do not want you putting yourself, or Meredith, in danger. Now, come have a cup of tea while you wait. Are you out of sorts this morning? I know you must be disappointed we will not have our ride, but there will be others."

"Disappointed? Why, of all the conceited—"

"Not disappointed? Then perhaps it is your concern for me that has put you in a temper. How flattering, but you really must not worry, Thea."

"I am *not* worried, Keswick, and I am not in a temper," she said furiously.

He grinned impudently, and after a moment she reluctantly smiled. "Very well. I own I am a trifle disturbed. Life was so peaceful until you returned, and now everything seems to be turning upside down."

He studied her for a moment, a frown furrowing his brow. "Should you like to take Meredith and go away for a bit? You could take her to London and show her some of the sights."

"Have I vexed you so much that you wish to be rid of me?" she asked, only half in jest. "Besides, Meredith would fight me tooth and nail if I tried to take her away from you."

"Meredith is fascinated with her new papa, but only for the moment and only because she never had me with her before. That will wear off soon enough. It is a very different thing than what she feels for you. If you were to leave, I fear she would judge me a sad replacement."

"Then we will not discuss my leaving," Althea said, feeling unusually in charity with him.

"Good. Keswick Manor would not be the same without you," he said, and carefully watched her face. He spoke more seriously than was his custom, but on seeing the astonishment in her eyes, he quickly retreated and added with a laugh, "Meredith would never forgive me if you left."

Althea endeavored to keep her voice as light as his. "The day may come, however. When you wed and bring your countess here, I shall be much in the way."

"I certainly hope not, Thea." He laughed suddenly and the sound seemed to fill the room, reverberating in her ears.

Althea arrived at the Braithwrites' farm with little knowledge of how she came to be there. She'd answered Meredith's questions during the ride, but not with conscious thought. She was preoccupied with Keswick and went over their conversation in her mind a dozen times. She did not know what to make of him, and she felt as though her emotions were running amok.

One moment she felt resentful, hating his return, and still much inclined to blame him for Deborah's death. The next, she was anxiously seeking his company, flattered by his attention, and feeling herself drawn by those laughing dark eyes. On more than one occasion she'd even caught herself wondering what it would be like to be kissed by him. She remembered the attraction she'd felt for him even while he was married to her cousin, and a blush of shame stole up her neck. Feeling disloyal to Deborah, she shook her head, making an effort to put thoughts of Keswick from her mind.

Mrs. Braithwrite bustled out of the house to greet them. She was a large woman, of ample proportions, and radiated good health. Her brown hair, liberally streaked with gray, was pulled into a knot at the back of her head although several strands escaped confinement. Her muscular arms bore mute testimony to the hard work she did and made Althea feel the veriest waif beside her.

Mrs. Braithwrite ushered her into the house with all due ceremony. She was given the best seat in the small parlor and the sons of the house were trotted out for her inspection. The Braithwrite boys ranged in age from four to sixteen and all seemed to take after their mama. Big lads with muscular bodies and happy dispositions, they did their mother proud. Hannah, the only daughter, looked, fortunately, like her papa. At fifteen she promised to be a beauty, with her slim figure, blond curls, and blue eyes.

Mrs. Braithwrite sent Hannah to bring in the dandelion wine for their guest. The youngest boy, Gilbert, toddled after her holding on to his sister's skirt. The rest of the boys begged permission to take Lady Meredith off with them to visit their newborn goat. Althea readily consented, knowing they would take good care of her charge. She watched them leave, envying the children their exuberance.

The odor of fresh baked bread filled the room, and Hannah soon returned with a heavily laden tray. Cheese was cut in large slabs and mounds of creamy butter rested beside the bread.

"Now, then, Miss Underwood, you have some of this. You're looking a mite peakish and thinner than I like to see you."

"Ma," her daughter wailed, "don't be embarrassing Miss Underwood that way. I think she looks perfect." She blushed at such a daring remark and looked down at her hands.

"Thank you, Hannah. It is kind of you to say so," Althea said, hoping to set the girl at ease. She turned to Mrs. Braithwrite with a warm smile. "Lord Keswick asked me to express his regrets. He particularly wished to visit you and charged me to bring some of your wine home to him."

Mrs. Braithwrite nodded. "We was looking for him yesterday and the boys were sore disappointed not to see him. He promised to have a look at that hog Todd is rearing. My boy thinks he'll take a blue ribbon at the fair this year."

Althea tried not to show her astonishment. The image of Keswick admiring a hog was beyond comprehension. She absently took a drink of the wine beside her, forgetting the potency of Mrs. Braithwrite's dandelion concoction. The raw liquid burned her throat. She gasped, trying desperately not to cough, and focused her attention on the older woman.

"Mama! Miss Underwood doesn't want to hear about Todd's old hog," Hannah was saying in an agony of embarrassment.

"Nothing wrong with hogs," her mama replied. "And it's the earl's business, miss. He ain't like some landlords only interested in the rents and revenues." To Althea she added, "Mr. Braithwrite is right pleased to have his lordship home again, seeing as how he means to make some improvements in the home farm. An absentee landlord ain't good for the farm, least that's what Mr. Braithwrite said. Not that Mr. Reading hasn't done a decent job, but a bailiff ain't the same as having his lordship here. We only hope he means to stay. Time past he was married again."

It was Althea's turn to blush at the look of inquiry Mrs. Braithwrite directed toward her. Hannah, too, stared at her with large, questioning eyes.

"I believe it's Lord Keswick's intention to remain at home," Althea managed to say, and sighed with relief as the boys trooped noisily in, Meredith happily in their midst. She was in raptures over the baby goat and instantly begged for one of her own. The conversation turned on the animals and the problems of farming, and the remainder of the visit passed serenely enough.

Althea and Meredith returned to Keswick Manor later that afternoon. They cantered into the stable yard and reined in their horses. An elaborate traveling carriage blocked the center of the yard. Althea was eyeing it curiously when Mason hurried out of the stables to help her dismount.

"Have we visitors?" she asked. "I do not believe I recognize the carriage."

"No, miss. I mean, yes, miss, we do have company, but no one I ever seen before. A young gentleman and his lady. They be friends of his lordship's. Prime cattle he's driving, Miss Underwood."

Althea nodded, her mind already busy planning for unexpected guests. If they were not from anywhere nearby, they would undoubtedly stay over, at least for one night. She hoped Mrs. Pennington had ordered bedchambers prepared.

Althea took Meredith in through the kitchen door and up the back stairs. It would not do to encounter their guests before she had a chance to tidy herself. She knew several strands of hair had escaped from her riding hat and the split-skirted habit was hardly proper attire for the drawing room. Miss Appletree met her in the upper hall.

"I am glad you are both back, Miss Underwood. Have they told you there are visitors? Lord Keswick sent word to bring Lady Meredith down as soon as you returned." She smiled, putting a hand on Meredith's head. "He is most anxious to show off his daughter."

"He would not be if he could see her now," Althea said, glancing ruefully down at Meredith. She had long since lost the ribbons from her hair and mud and grass vied for prominence on her habit. "Will you see her properly dressed while I change? I shall not be long."

Miss Appletree agreed, then hesitated.

"Was there something else?" Althea asked, anxious to get to her bedchamber.

"It may be presumptuous of me, but . . . Well, it is only I saw the couple arrive and they are a most elegant pair. I should not be surprised if the lady's ensemble just arrived from Paris."

Althea smiled. "And you feared I would don one of my old morning dresses and be cast in the shade?"

The governess reddened, but the truth was, Althea seldom dressed as befitted her station. She did not have a vain bone in her body and was too much concerned with other matters to pay attention to her dress and her hair. The problem was gentlemen, as a rule, could not be depended on to differentiate between true gold and mere gilding— and the young lady in the drawing room was dressed to the teeth.

Still, she was not sorry she had spoken and

105

openly expressed her approval when Miss Underwood came to collect Lady Meredith an hour later. Gone was the raffish-looking gamine. Althea wore a simply cut half-dress of deep gold with an overdress of amber muslin. Tiny seed pearls decorated the sleeves and bodice and a gold ribbon accentuated the high waist. Her hair was swept up in a becoming fall of curls tied with another gold ribbon. Miss Appletree thought she looked entirely sweet and charming.

Meredith, too, approved. "You look so pretty, Aunt Thea," she cried at once, making Althea wonder if she'd been too careless of late with her appearance.

She knelt to kiss Meredith. "Thank you, darling. You look very pretty, too. Your papa will be most proud of you. Now let us go meet our guests."

"I'll come and collect her in a few moments," Miss Appletree promised, before cautioning Lady Meredith to mind her manners. She superstitiously crossed her fingers, hoping her impulsive charge would not do or say anything to disgrace her.

Althea, with Meredith in hand, paused outside the drawing room. Straightening the ribbon in Meredith's hair, she heard the high-pitched feminine voice of their visitor float across the room.

"It was so frightfully dull after you left, Andrew, and the princess behaved more outrageously each day. I cannot tell you how much I longed for dear, civilized England."

Althea stepped into the drawing room. The young lady was seated demurely enough on the sofa, but her eyes were devouring Keswick. Althea fancied it was not England the woman longed for but rather a particular Englishman.

Keswick, catching sight of Althea and Meredith, managed to get to his feet with the aid of a cane. The young gentleman on his left stood at once and the lady more slowly. The introductions were made, and Althea took the measure of Louise Demont, silently giving thanks to Miss Appletree for her warning. The lady was indeed dressed in the height of fashion and had the figure to carry off her stunning blue carriage dress with aplomb. Blond hair fell in neat ringlets beneath curled ostrich plumes dyed to match Miss Demont's dress. Large blue eyes, heavily fringed with dark lashes, returned Althea's appraisal.

"So you are the kind cousin who looks after Andrew's little daughter. He spoke of you often when we were abroad."

Althea's glance flew to Keswick.

"I only said how good it was of you to stay on here and care for Meredith."

"And this must be the precious Lady Meredith? Let me see you, my dear child," Miss Demont commanded.

Meredith suffered a sudden attack of shyness and hid behind Althea's skirts.

"Make your curtsy to the Demonts," Althea whispered to her.

Meredith peered around Althea at her papa, who encouraged her with a warm smile. She stepped forward then and made a graceful curtsy.

Perry Demont took her tiny hand and bowed over it. "I am charmed to meet you, Lady Meredith."

"She certainly bears a marked resemblance to

you, Andrew," said Miss Demont, eyeing the little girl uncertainly. She was one of those people who hadn't the knack of dealing with children, and she knew they sensed it. She knelt down, careful not to muss her dress. "I came especially to see you, my dear. Your papa talked about you a great deal. If it were not for you, he would still be traveling with us."

Meredith retreated to Althea's side and took hold of her hand tightly. Althea could not understand it. Meredith was never this shy with strangers. If anything, the child had too much poise for her age. She excused herself and took Meredith with her into the hall.

"Do you want to go back upstairs with Miss Appletree?" she asked her quietly.

Meredith nodded, head down.

Althea knelt beside her, taking both her hands in her own. "Are you afraid of Miss Demont, darling?"

Meredith shook her head, her curls swinging. Her dark eyes, so like Keswick's, glared at the closed door. "I do not like the way she looks at Papa."

Althea was nonplussed. What could she say?

"Will Papa go away again, Aunt Thea?"

She hugged the child to her. "No, darling. Miss Demont and her brother are only here for a visit. You run along and see what Buttons is doing and do not worry about your papa. Tell Miss Appletree I excused you."

Althea returned to the drawing room to find their guests discussing their stay abroad.

"I met the Demonts when I was in Italy," Keswick explained to her when they were all sitting down again.

"We were all houseguests at the Villa d'Este in Como," Miss Demont added. At Althea's questioning look she elaborated, "Surely even in this backwater you have heard of Princess Caroline's Italian villa? I quite thought it was the talk of England."

"Perhaps Miss Underwood is not given to gossip," Perry Demont suggested, his eyes clearly showing his admiration. He was slightly taller than his sister but of the same slender build. He wore a fierce mustache and his merry blue eyes gave him the look of an adventurer.

"I fear I am no better than the rest of my gender, sir. Our village seems to thrive on the scandals the princess brews, although I did not connect the name of the villa for a moment." She turned to Keswick with a mischievous grin. "You never told us you were a guest of the princess, sir. Lady Penhallow will be green with envy."

Miss Demont laughed, a soft, musical trill. "Do not look to Andrew to gossip about the princess. He was her champion, you know, and would not hear a word against her."

Keswick looked uncomfortable and suggested tea. He pulled the bell rope, but Louise Demont continued to tease him. "Princess Caroline was most fond of him and even offered him the use of her villa while she was traveling. One wonders what would have happened if she were not so infatuated with Pergami."

"Pergami? Is he the Italian baron she made her chamberlain?" Althea asked, intrigued.

"Oh, my dear, he is much more than that. He is with her constantly and is even admitted to her chambers while she is dressing. She cooks for him, too. She makes no secret of it. Indeed, she tells all the world that Italian men know how to treat a woman."

"Perhaps she does so because her own subjects have treated her so badly," Keswick said tartly.

"You see?" Louis gestured to Althea. "You see how he defends her? It was the same in Italy. No one must say a word against the princess."

"Lord Keswick may be wiser than you, Louise," her brother warned. "Caroline will be our queen one day and I fancy she will remember all those who abused her."

"Oh, he does not care for that, do you, Andrew?"

Althea wondered if it was the pain in his ankle or distaste for the conversation that caused the grimace on Keswick's face. He stretched his leg out, frowning, before replying, "I feel sorry for the princess. Beneath all the face paint she wears and those atrocious wigs is a very lonely and frightened young woman."

"And I suppose you think it fitting behavior for her to drive through the streets in that ridiculous carriage shaped like a shell, with grooms in pink tights and spangles?" There was venom in Louise's voice and Althea glanced from her to Keswick.

"It *was* a ludicrous sight," Perry offered, trying to ease the tension. He turned to Althea. "She has grown as fat as the Regent and she lies in her carriage with much of her body exposed. Her gowns are always indecently low cut and she drives with her skirts up to her knees so that one sees her short, chubby legs. It is not a sight to inspire one's devotion."

"And with that horrid little boy she adopted lolling beside her," Louise added, her voice laden with disgust. "If, indeed, he is not her own son as rumor has it. She takes him everywhere with her."

"It was proven the child was adopted," Keswick reminded her. "Do you really wonder at it, Louise? She loves children and was kept from her own daughter. When Princess Charlotte died, she was devastated. That little boy is the only soul in the world who truly loves her."

"Andrew, I vow you are even worse now than you were when we were at the villa. The princess is not the first woman to lose her child."

Althea stared at her, stunned by such a callous attitude. Princess Caroline's faults may have been legion, but any woman who had lost a child deserved some measure of sympathy.

Perry, too, seemed disconcerted by his sister's attitude and tried to pass it off. "When you marry, my dear, and have your own child, you will understand better the bond between mother and child." He turned to Althea with a smile. "You seem very attached to Lady Meredith, Miss Underwood. No doubt you are more sympathetic toward our princess?"

"The idea of ever losing Meredith does not bear thinking of. Perhaps we should speak of something else."

"It is best you face it, Miss Underwood," Louise advised, directing a fond look at the earl. "When Andrew marries—"

Keswick knocked against the table with his cane when he tried to rise too quickly. "Althea, would you see what's keeping tea? It's an age since I rang."

Althea rose, glad of an excuse to leave the room.

She felt uncomfortably warm and paused outside the door to compose herself. The murmur of low voices drifted into the hall, the words indistinguishable. What had Louise Demont been about to say? The possessive manner in which she'd looked at Keswick, the caressing way she had used his name, hinted at an intimacy beyond mere friendship. Could there be an understanding between them?

Althea felt sick. She could not bear it if Keswick married the woman. Of course, her concern was all for Meredith's sake. Louise Demont was the sort who would do everything possible to come between Keswick and his daughter. It mattered not that she herself found the woman repulsive, Althea told herself. But a small inner voice persisted in declaring that Meredith was not the only reason for her concern.

She had no time to analyze her feelings. A footman was coming down the hall with the tea tray, Aunt Pysie hard on his heels.

"Althea dear, I understand we have visitors. Friends of Andrew's? How diverting for him when he is laid up. It is so vexing to have nothing to do and no one to talk with. Of course, I do not mean to imply you are not good company, but one needs new faces now and then, do you not agree?"

Althea smiled, glad Aunt Pysie had returned. She started to follow the older woman into the drawing room when a tiny mew attracted her attention. Her kitten peeped around the hall from his place on the stairs. He gave another louder cry and she turned her steps to pick him up.

"What are you doing lurking in the hall?" she asked, scratching him behind the ears. "You were not invited to tea today. We have guests, you know, and one cat among us is quite enough." Now that was unworthy of me, she thought, but a smile teased the corners of her mouth. The footman returned to the hall and she thrust the kitten into his arms.

"Would you take Mr. Bows to the kitchen, Frank, and see that he has a large dish of cream?" The kitten purred as though he understood and Althea entered the drawing room in a better humor.

"There you are, Althea," Aunt Pysie said from her place on the sofa beside her nephew. "I was just telling Miss Demont I could not imagine what was detaining you."

Perry Demont rose at once and drew up another chair for Althea, and Aunt Pysie handed her a cup of tea.

"I am sorry I was delayed," Althea replied, smiling. "Mr. Bows was in the hall and, as usual, demanded attention."

"A rather strange sort of name," Perry drawled, looking over his teacup. His blue eyes danced as if he sensed a joke.

"Mr. Bows is a white kitten. One, I might add, who has been extremely spoiled ever since his lordship brought him home," she explained with an unusually warm smile for Keswick.

"A kitten! Oh, how quaint," Louise said. "Really, Andrew, you have become unbelievably domesticated. Your friends in Paris and Rome would laugh uproariously if they could see you now."

"You do not know the half of it," Althea murmured sweetly. "His lordship has become an expert on husbandry as well." She spoke directly to

Keswick. "Young Todd Braithwrite was sorely disappointed you were unable to visit his hog today."

Aunt Pysie hastily offered to refill Miss Demont's cup, which the lady had barely touched. Keswick grinned and Perry sat back, hugely enjoying the exchange.

"A *hog*? Surely you jest, Miss Underwood?" Louise hunched her slender shoulders in a shiver of revulsion.

"Indeed not. The animal belongs to one of Keswick's tenants. He stands on excellent terms with the entire family. Which reminds me, my lord, Todd's mother sent the dandelion wine you requested. She is certain it will have a salubrious effect on your ankle."

Louise was seen to shudder delicately.

"No, Andrew, no," Aunt Pysie muttered. "Really, I cannot advise it. I have nothing to say against Mrs. Braithwrite. I am sure she is a very good woman in her way, but she makes the worst wine in the county. I cannot think it would be good for you."

"I did promise I would sample it," Keswick said with a straight face.

"You are much too good to your tenants," his aunt replied. "If you wish to build them new roofs and rotate the crops, or whatever it is you were talking of doing, it is all well and good. But drinking dandelion wine is carrying your duty to excess. No one would expect it of you."

"Except Althea," he said, and held her gaze with an intimacy apparent to everyone in the room.

She lowered her own eyes, pretending an inordinate interest in her cup of tea.

Perry chuckled loudly. "Come, my dear sister. I think it is time we took our leave."

Althea's eyes flew open. "Surely you are not departing so soon, Mr. Demont? We have rooms prepared for you and anticipated you would stay the night."

"Thank you, Miss Underwood, but I do not believe there is any point in our remaining." His blue eyes met hers with an understanding look that brought a blush to her cheeks. He turned to his sister. "You do agree with me, do you not, Louise?"

She rose stiffly, giving him her hand. "Behave yourself, Perry." She turned to Althea. "We are promised to Lord Firth and really must take our leave while there is still light."

Keswick rose and stood leaning on his cane. Louise turned and gave him her hand. He managed to bow and place a light kiss on the gloved fingers. "I am delighted you found time to visit, Louise, although I did warn you how it would be."

"You did, Andrew," she said with a reluctant smile. "By faith, I never would have believed it. The most sophisticated man on the continent turned into a country bumpkin, with hogs no less. When I see the princess again, I shall tell her. She will enjoy it immensely, I am sure."

Perry shook hands with him, too, and made his bow to Aunt Pysie. Althea walked with them to the door. Louise was anxious to be gone, but Perry lingered for a moment, holding Althea's hand captive in his.

"I told my sister how it would be, but she would not believe me. She quite thought that after a month of rusticating, Keswick would be more than ready to return to more civilized society."

"You are very perceptive, sir."

"Perhaps, but I fear I had an unfair advantage. I helped take care of Andrew when he was wounded. He was delirious for a time and called out one name over and over."

"Meredith?" she asked, sincerely touched by the thought.

"Althea," he corrected, and was gone before she could say a word.

Chapter 7

Althea entered the south drawing room from the garden doors with a basket of freshly cut roses on her arm. She intended to refresh the floral arrangements, which were looking sadly wilted from the unusual heat. She paused just inside the door, her nose wrinkling in dismay. A putrid aroma filled the room. She sniffed. It smelled like hardboiled eggs gone bad. Dozens of them.

Setting her basket down, Althea opened both doors to the garden and took a deep breath of the fresh air. Then she followed her nose. The strange odor seemed to be coming from the kitchen. She could not imagine their chef cooking anything that smelled so atrocious. He was a Frenchman and a veritable master of culinary art.

The kitchen door swung open and Althea was almost bowled over by Chef Bernard. He rushed past her, hands gesturing violently and a steady stream of French spewing from his lips. Most of what he muttered was incomprehensible to Althea, but she understood the tone, if not the actual words. Their fat, little chef was extremely agitated. She heard other voices raised in the kitchen and hurried inside.

Aunt Pysie, enveloped in one of Bernard's huge

aprons, stood in front of the long trestle table, tears running down her cheeks. Three scullery maids, aprons pulled up to their eyes, huddled a few feet away. The two assistant cooks were nowhere to be seen. Althea felt her own eyes stinging and raised a lace handkerchief to her nose.

Aunt Pysie caught sight of her. "Oh, my dear girl, I am glad you have come. There is something quite dreadfully wrong with this recipe and I cannot think what," she said, staring at the offending vessel.

Althea made an effort to speak without breathing. "What on earth are you making? The entire house reeks."

"It is not so bad once you become accustomed to it," Aunt Pysie defended, swiping at the tears running down her cheeks. "It is Eugenia Yardley's recipe. A specific for gout and rheumatism, only I cannot believe that she ever made something that smelled so horridly. Surely it would have been commented on, and I distinctly recollect Eugenia's house always smelled wonderfully."

"Are you certain you have the right recipe?" Althea asked, edging closer for a better look. She had not thought it possible, but the vile concoction looked even worse than it smelled.

Aunt Pysie gestured to the cloth-covered journal lying on the table. "You may see for yourself. It's all there in Eugenia's own hand. You may not remember, but everyone in this county used to swear by the Yardley Specific. Eugenia promised me the recipe even though Lady Penhallow pressed her for it. I intended to write the directions out several years ago, but then Eugenia died so suddenly I never had the opportunity. In truth, I had forgotten it entirely until Lady Fielding told me poor Sir Edward is suffering dreadfully from the gout. She said she was certain he would recover quickly if only she had the Yardley Specific."

"If this is a sample of her curative, it is little wonder Mrs. Yardley passed on," Althea said in a high voice as she pressed her handkerchief over her nose. She picked up the journal and backed off several feet.

"Really, Althea, have you no respect for the dead? Besides, Eugenia died of the ague as you must very well know, and I was never more vexed because she forgot to give me the recipe."

Althea retreated to the kitchen door and studied the spidery handwriting in the journal. She barely heard her aunt.

"She thought someone should have it as she was moving to Essex to live with her daughter. Of course I inquired afterward, when they were packing up her belongings, but no one knew what had become of her things. I had quite resigned myself to the curative being lost to us, and then, what do you suppose? Only last week I received a parcel from Maria Rotterdean, bless her. She found her mama's journal in an old trunk and wrote at once, knowing I should like to have it."

"I wonder she did not keep it herself," Althea said.

Pysie gave the brew one last hopeful look before trotting to Althea's side. "I had to pay two shillings postal charges, too, and now it is all a dreadful waste."

"I think I see the problem, Aunt Pysie," Althea said, a smile tugging at the corners of her mouth.

She indicated the journal page. "See, the recipe begins here."

"Of course, dear. It says so right there. 'Specific for the Cure of Rheumatism and Gout.' I promise you I followed the directions most exactly."

The first few items listed were unexceptional, and Aunt Pysie read them off. "'A dozen eggs allowed to age for three days, the juice of six lemons and half again as much vinegar, six onions peeled and chopped, and two garlic leaves.'"

"That part is straight enough, dear one. It is when you turned the page that you ran into trouble. See? These two pages are stuck together." Althea carefully separated the brittle sheets. "Instead of the specific, you were adding the ingredients for 'An Effective Deterrent to Rid the Cellars of Rats and Other Vermin.'"

"Vermin? Oh, my. No wonder it smells so dreadfully. I expect it was the hog's dung. I must say I did wonder at that."

Althea laughed. "Never tell me you actually went out and collected hog's dung?"

"No, of course not, dear. I sent the second footman, although I did think a bucketful sounded excessive." She could not see what was so amusing in that to set Althea laughing again and said so.

"Never mind, Aunt Pysie. Our priority now must be to restore the kitchen and air the house before Keswick returns."

"I *have* returned and demand to know what's afoot. This place smells worse than a pig sty," Keswick said, striding into the kitchen. The scullery maids stood gawking at him and giggling beneath their aprons.

"Aunt Pysie was making a specific, my lord, and

the recipe went a trifle awry," Althea answered with a straight face. Keswick's unbelieving look set her off again. She laughed so hard she could barely speak, but managed to gasp, "I fear it was the *hog's dung*."

Aunt Pysie looked offended. "I assure you, Andrew, it was a mistake such as could happen to anyone. And I should like to know who was so careless as to allow the pages to become stuck together. I have a good mind to write Maria and demand she reimburse me the two shillings I paid."

"Come into the garden, Keswick, and I shall explain," Althea said, taking pity on his confusion.

He crossed the kitchen in a few steps, no longer requiring a cane. In the last week his ankle seemed to have healed completely. He took her arm, anxious to be out of the foul-smelling kitchen.

Althea paused at the door to direct one of the maids. "Take that crock out to the gardeners and have them bury it somewhere." Then, yielding to the urgent pressure on her arm, she walked with Keswick through the kitchen garden and across the stone path to the rose garden. With the return to fresh air came the constraint she felt in his presence. She had avoided being alone with him ever since the Demonts' visit several days past. Now she was intensely aware of his hand beneath her elbow and the very masculine scent he exuded. She smiled suddenly.

"A private joke, Althea, or will you share it?" he asked, seating her on a rustic bench.

"I was only thinking you smell much better than the kitchen, if you would know the truth."

He laughed, sitting down close beside her. "Scant

praise, that. I never smelled anything so vile. Not even when Filmore and I trapped a skunk."

Althea explained what had gone wrong with the recipe. When she mentioned the hog's dung, infectious laughter bubbled within her. Keswick, as she had known he would, chuckled appreciatively, his eyes crinkling with amusement.

"Only Aunt Pysie could have made such a mistake!"

"I know, but please do not tease her, Keswick. She is truly upset. Lady Penhallow's nose would have been quite out of joint if Aunt Pysie had succeeded with the specific."

"Egad, does that mean she will try again? Perhaps I can get my hands on the wretched journal and burn the thing."

"Your present task, sir, is to find Bernard and placate him somehow."

"Must I?" His words were innocent enough, but his eyes seemed to be saying something quite different.

"You must," she said, glancing away uneasily. "Unless you wish your aunt to cook our dinner tonight?"

"I shall find him. Lord only knows what Aunt Pysie would serve us. Have we guests coming again?" His voice was teasing, almost caressing, and she dared not look at him.

Althea had the uncomfortable notion that Keswick knew precisely what she'd been about. Perry Demont's last words had shaken her. Uncertain of Keswick's feelings, even more unsure of her own, she had deliberately avoided being alone with him by filling the house with dinner guests. Her ploy had succeeded, but she knew she could not continue to avoid him.

"No, we dine *en famille* this evening," she remarked after a lengthy pause.

Keswick watched her profile. He did not need to see her eyes to know she was ill at ease. A slight blush delicately stained her cheeks. Rising to his feet, he offered her a hand, saying lightly, "It is fortunate, I suppose. I doubt we could explain the smell without embarrassing Aunt Pysie. I believe she needs something to occupy her mind."

"She has been rather restless of late," Althea agreed, glad to change the subject.

"I have a project in mind that should keep her busy. We will discuss it at dinner. Now, if you will see what you can do to air the house, I shall try to find our missing chef."

Keswick left her alone near the kitchen garden. Chiding herself for the ridiculous surge of disappointment she felt, Althea returned to the kitchen and set the maids to airing the room. Footmen were directed to open every door and window.

Leaving them to their tasks, she hurried to her room and changed into her riding habit. The breeze blowing in off Derwent Water would help dilute the stench in the house. Perhaps, she thought, it would also help blow the cobwebs from her mind.

There was no news of Grimsby, Mason told her gloomily, as he saddled her mare a few minutes later. He led the horse out, calling over his shoulder for young Johns to saddle up as well.

"No," Althea ordered. "I will not be riding far and I do not need a groom with me."

"But his lordship said as 'ow you weren't to ride out alone—"

"No groom, Mason," she interrupted as he gave her a leg up. "I shall return within the hour." She pulled her horse's head to the right and cantered down the drive before he could protest further.

Mason shook his head and directed young Johns to go after her. "Stay far enough back so Miss Underwood don't see you, understand? His lordship will have our 'eads if 'en something was to happen to 'er."

Althea was annoyed when she caught sight of Johns following her, but she gave no sign of it, deciding instead to give him a ride to remember. When she reached the long stretch of open pasture, she gave the mare her head and raced across the field. She reached the far end in record time and took the fence there with ease. Her horse was slightly winded and the ribbons of her hat had come undone, tangling her hair, but she felt better for the gallop. Dismounting and carrying her hat in hand, she led the mare down a dirt path to a small clearing in the grove of trees. It was an ideal place for a picnic. She had brought Meredith there numerous times.

Althea tied the horse to a willow tree before seating herself on top of a large boulder. From there she had an excellent view of Derwent Water and for several moments she sat and stared at the lake. Loosening the pins in her hair, she allowed the breeze to brush it back from her head. Her hair was as tangled as her emotions. She knew she must come to terms with her feelings about Keswick. The man utterly confused her.

Althea was too engrossed in her own thoughts to

hear another horse approach. The rider was only a few yards distant when her horse nickered to his stallion. She looked about, startled.

Lord Filmore. Black suited him, she thought, watching him dismount. Tall and lean, he moved with the grace of a large cat. The sort that stalked the woods at night, preying on smaller beasts. He tethered his horse next to her own and crossed the clearing before addressing her.

"Miss Underwood? I rather thought it was you. I saw you from the woods."

"Lord Filmore," she said, and nodded in acknowl-edgment. "I heard you had returned. How do you do?" The question was merely polite and Althea slid from her perch to stand facing him. She was barely acquainted with the man and had not seen him for over five years. Those years had not been kind to him, she thought. A bleakness had settled about his eyes and heavy lines were etched be-tween his dark brows.

"Well enough," he answered briefly, his gray eyes raking over her. "I thought perhaps you'd taken a spill. I did not see your mount until I came down the hill."

"It was kind of you to be concerned, sir," she re-plied, acutely conscious of her disheveled appear-ance. "I suppose I must have looked rather odd sitting here. I confess I was daydreaming."

"And I have intruded. My apologies," he an-swered gravely, turning to leave.

"Wait," Althea cried impulsively.

Filmore turned back, surprise arching his black brows.

Althea reddened, wondering briefly what had prompted her to detain him. She struggled to find some words. "I ... It has been such a long time since we have seen you, sir. Please stay for a moment. Tell me what brings you home again."

He stepped closer, towering above her. Althea almost lost her nerve, but this was a chance to find out if Filmore intended harm to Keswick. She summoned all her courage and her brown eyes went up to meet his directly.

"You should not be out here alone, Miss Underwood," he said at last. "I can imagine what Keswick would have to say if he knew."

"Lord Keswick is not my keeper. Besides," she added with a sudden impish grin, "I am not alone. There is a young groom in the woods over there. He follows me most discreetly and thinks I do not know."

Filmore smiled for just an instant. Brief though it was, it softened the hard planes of his face and gave her heart. She gestured toward the boulder. "May I offer you a seat, sir?"

He bowed. "After you, Miss Underwood."

When they were both comfortably situated, Althea waved toward Derwent Water. "Whenever I feel troubled I ride out here. There is something about the vastness of the water that makes my problems seem rather insignificant."

He nodded his understanding and they sat without speaking for several minutes.

When Filmore finally spoke, he bit off the words as though they were being pulled from his soul. "I used to come here when I was a boy. With Andrew."

"Keswick told me you were very close once," she prodded quietly.

"I loved him like a brother."

126

There was such poignant longing and despair in his voice, Althea's heart ached for him. He was still in mourning, but she wondered suddenly if it was for Oliver or for his lost friendship with Keswick.

She laid a gentle hand on his arm in understanding. "I was very close to my cousin and can understand a little how you must feel. It was Deborah who showed this spot to me. Keswick brought her here once, but she thought it too damp."

"I remember her. She was taller than you, I believe, but she seemed very fragile. Almost ethereal. I was sorry to hear about her passing. It must have been difficult for you."

"It was. Deborah and I were raised together and, because I was the elder, I looked after her. When she died, I felt as if I had somehow failed her." She hesitated and then added quietly, "For a long time I blamed Keswick."

"He has a great deal to answer for," Filmore said, the words sounding hard and flat.

"Perhaps," she agreed softly. "When Deborah first died, I felt very angry and rather helpless. I blamed myself. I thought there was something more I could have done to protect her. Then I began blaming Keswick." She paused, trying to judge his reaction. Filmore continued to stare out at the water, unblinking. Not a muscle moved in his face. She could not be sure he was even listening.

Althea took a deep breath. "I have been sitting here thinking of my cousin. We were very close and I loved her dearly, but I have come to realize no one was to blame for her death. She never had the will to deal with her life. Poor Deborah was too afraid to live."

"Keswick made her that way."

"No, I do not believe so. She was afraid of . . . oh, everything, her entire life."

He turned to face her. "You are wrong. I saw your cousin, Miss Underwood, on several occasions. I saw the way she feared him."

"Oh, yes, she was indeed fearful of Keswick. I saw it myself. But do you not see? Deborah would have been afraid of anyone she married. It is probably heathen in me to say so, but I believe she was somehow meant to die young and there was nothing that any of us could do to prevent it. It was her . . . her destiny."

He turned his head away. There was a long silence, the gentle lapping of the water in the distance the only sound.

She tried again. "Deborah would not have wanted me to grieve for her forever. She told me once she admired my courage."

Filmore stirred and slid off the boulder. His face had grown hard again and Althea drew back against the rock when she saw the thinly veiled fury in his eyes.

"I am glad, for your sake, that you have come to terms with your cousin's death, Miss Underwood. It *was* your cousin we were speaking of, was it not?"

"Partially," she said, her eyes admitting the truth. "Keswick was no more to blame for her death than he was for your brother's—"

Jack Filmore turned away, abruptly shutting off her words. He climbed the path in stony silence, mounted, and rode off without a backward glance.

Halfway through dinner Althea lifted a glass of peach ratafia in mock salute to Keswick. "I salute your tact and diplomacy, my lord."

He looked wary. "Drop the other shoe, Thea."

She laughed. "I am quite sincere, Keswick. You should be commended for your handling of our chef. This is quite the best dinner he has ever produced. The turtle soup was delicious, the pheasant unusually tender, and this chicken dish is superb. Whatever did you say to him?"

"We merely spoke of some of the places I visited while in Paris like the Hotel d'Espagne in the rue de Seine. Bernard now understands that I have a basis from which to judge his art." He motioned to a footman. "Please convey my compliments to the chef. Tell him the chicken Marengo is the best I have ever tasted."

"Is that what it is called?" Aunt Pysie asked, wrinkling her nose. "It smells distinctly of garlic."

Keswick leaned back in his chair, sipping a glass of port. He was in an expansive mood and nodded to his aunt. "Rumor has it the dish was first served to Napoleon after his victory at Marengo. He liked the taste so well, he ordered his chef to prepare it after every battle."

"I daresay he did," she said, sampling another bite. "Doubtless he would have liked anything after fasting for several days. But do you think we should actually serve it to guests, Andrew?"

"Why ever not, Aunt Pysie?" Althea asked. "I am sure our neighbors would enjoy it."

"But, my dear—*Napoleon's* favorite dish? The

man was quite mad, and after the way he behaved, well, I am certain Lady Penhallow would consider it unpatriotic of us."

Keswick laughed aloud. "Do not give it a thought. If Lady Penhallow objects, you may tell her chicken Marengo is one of the Regent's favorite dishes. You might even set a trend."

While Aunt Pysie considered the merits of such a notion, the plates were removed and replaced with an assortment of cakes, tarts, cheeses, and fruit. She looked at the large variety and sighed. "If Bernard continues to set such a table, I fear you will fall prey to gout, Andrew. We shall have need of Eugenia Yardley's specific after all."

Keswick looked alarmed and quickly gestured to a footman to remove his plate. "No, I promise you I shall not overindulge. More to the point, I fear you will be too occupied to have time for making any curatives. I have been considering hosting a ball."

"A ball? But, Andrew, the ballroom has not been used in years and years. You know the west wing is shut up. Your papa, God rest his soul, said it was much too dangerous to use. The wood has rotted and goodness knows what else after all this time."

"Aunt Pysie is right, Keswick. The door to that wing is bricked shut. It must be twenty years since anyone has been in there."

"Not quite. I opened it yesterday and looked about. A great deal of repair is needed, but I believe it's time the wing was restored."

"Andrew, never tell me you went in there alone," Aunt Pysie begged, fanning her breast. "Why, you might have been hurt and we would never have known."

"I had Evans with me, as well as several footmen, so you need not be alarmed. The ballroom is not as bad as I recollected. The floor must be replaced, of course, and I fear the great chandelier is working loose."

"The chandelier? Good heavens, I have not thought of the tradition in years. I was just a girl when your grandfather announced the engagement of your father to Cecelia Hatfield."

"Tradition?" Althea asked, puzzled.

"My great-grandfather brought the chandelier back with him from Italy and it has always hung in the ballroom. It weighs at least twelve stone and holds above a hundred candles. It should look magnificent when it is cleaned and properly hung. If you would care to see it, I will show it to you tomorrow morning."

"I've heard tales of the grand balls given at Keswick Manor, but what is the tradition Aunt Pysie mentioned?"

"Whenever the heir became officially engaged, a huge ball was given to mark the occasion and a painting commissioned of the bride. The portrait of my mother hanging in the long gallery was completed right after her ball. The gown is the same one she wore when her betrothal was announced. Sir Thomas Lawrence attended the ball and stayed as a guest here until her portrait was finished."

"It is bad luck to break a tradition," Aunt Pysie said, finishing off a tart. "Only look what happened to Deborah—" She broke off, realizing her *faux pas.* "Althea, my dear, I am sorry. I was not thinking."

A shadow passed across her eyes, but Althea managed to smile. "Deborah would never have wished for a ball in her honor. And it would have been decidedly difficult for Keswick's father to have given her one."

"Decidedly," Keswick seconded, smiling at her efforts. "Considering that at the time Papa had been in the ground for better than seven years, I would even say impossible. Only imagine what Lady Penhallow would have thought had he returned."

"Andrew, you should never jest about such a thing, but I am glad you are going to have dear Deborah's portrait done."

Althea dropped her fork. "Deborah's portrait?"

"Oh, dear. I have spoiled your surprise, haven't I?" Aunt Pysie said, looking aghast at her nephew.

To Althea's astonishment, Keswick looked embarrassed. "It was to be a gift for your birthday next month," he said, motioning to the footman to refill his glass. "I commissioned Bradley Holmes to paint it from a miniature your uncle gave me. Holmes is not so well known as Lawrence, but I think he will be, given time. But you shall judge for yourself. He will be here next week to start work on it."

"Goodness, an artist staying in the house and a ball to plan. We shall be at sixes and sevens for the next few weeks," his aunt said, looking pleased at the thought.

"It will mean a great deal of work for you both," Keswick cautioned. "I want everything to be first-rate. Bernard will be in charge of the food, but you shall have to work out the menu with him. And I want you both to have new gowns. I have engaged a modiste to come down from London to fit you."

He looked absurdly pleased with himself and although Althea smiled at his enthusiasm, she wondered what was behind this sudden desire to host a ball. "Have you some special date in mind, Keswick?"

"If I can get the work done, and I think it possible, then the ball will be in six weeks' time. It shall be the final celebration of the summer. I leave the decorations and planning to you ladies, but do not restrain yourselves. Be as extravagant as you please. Invite everyone in the county."

"Gracious, Andrew, we shall have to begin at once, and the entire house will have to be turned out. Some of the families will overnight and the rooms must be cleaned thoroughly. Oh, dear, I do not know if six weeks will be enough time."

"Engage more maids, Aunt Pysie, more footmen—whatever you need. No expense is to be spared."

Althea watched him closely. Keswick had something more in mind than celebrating the end of summer, she was certain of it. There was a look of devilment in his eyes, and his lips were set in the half smile she'd come to know so well.

Sensing her regard, Keswick glanced at her, his dark eyes full of amusement. He lifted his wineglass in a salute. "I hope, I very much hope, to make a special announcement at the ball."

"What sort of announcement, Andrew?" Aunt

Pysie demanded. "What mischief have you afoot?"

"I cannot say more as yet, my dearest aunt, but I hope you will both be most pleased."

Chapter 8

Althea awoke Saturday morning with a dull, aching head, which did not improve as the morning progressed. Keswick's laborers had arrived at an early hour and filled the house with a relentless din. Her normal routine overset, it seemed to Althea that no matter where she turned, she encountered carpenters and plasterers. The sound of vigorous hammering even invaded the breakfast room, making conversation all but impossible. Althea, with a hopeless gesture to Aunt Pysie, fled to the nursery wing. She intended to escape the general madness by taking Meredith with her into the village.

Miss Appletree met her in the upper hall. Althea's heart sank when she saw the worried frown on the governess's normally serene countenance.

"Lady Meredith is complaining of a sore throat, and I fear she is a little feverish. She has been asking for you continuously."

Althea followed her down the hall to Meredith's room. She shut the door carefully, blocking out most of the racket coming from the west wing. Meredith was sitting up in bed. When she saw Althea, she immediately lifted her arms up in a pitiful gesture. Althea quickly crossed the room and enveloped the child in a hug. Meredith's brow felt overly warm against her own cool cheek. She drew back and tenderly wiped the tears from the child's face.

"Now what is this? Your papa will not think his little princess so pretty if her eyes are all red from crying."

"Aunt Thea, my voice hurts," Meredith complained in a raspy croak. Her tiny face was flushed and her eyes looked feverish. Even her hair seemed to have lost some of its luster and lay in tangles.

"Of course it does, darling. I think you have caught a summer cold. Suppose we have Dr. Mayhew come see you? He will give you something to make you feel better."

Meredith shook her head, clutching Althea tightly. "I want *you* to stay with me."

"I shall, pet, but I want you to see Dr. Mayhew, too." She turned to the governess. "Please send someone to fetch the doctor and then ask Aunt Pysie to send up some fresh milk."

"I don't want any milk," Meredith cried.

"I know, darling," Althea consoled her, smoothing the dark curls away from the child's brow. "Shall I brush your hair for you?"

Meredith refused as she refused every suggestion offered. She was cross, fidgety, and would not allow Althea out of her sight. She complained she was thirsty and then would not drink anything. It hurt to swallow, she protested, tears flowing.

Dr. Mayhew's arrival was greeted with howls of protest. Usually his jovial manner was enough to induce a smile in his smaller patients, but not today. Meredith clung to Althea, hiding her face and whimpering. It took the doctor a grueling half hour to examine her. Meredith resisted him with every ounce of her tiny body.

She cried loudly when Althea left her side to confer with the doctor in the hall.

"There's no need to be unduly alarmed, Miss Underwood," he said, raising his voice above the din of hammering and Meredith's sobs. "She will be feverish for a day or two. See that she rests in bed for a few days and try to keep her quiet. The fever will run its course and Lady Meredith should be back to normal by the end of the week."

"Thank you, Dr. Mayhew. I am sorry she was so troublesome."

"Do not give it a thought. I have had worse patients." Adjusting his spectacles, he peered at her closely. "You look unusually tired yourself. Are you feeling quite the thing?"

"It has been a difficult morning, sir. I have a bit of the headache, no more," she replied, smiling. "Lord Keswick is restoring the west wing, as you can hear."

"Indeed. Well, try to get some rest yourself and do not attempt to nurse Lady Meredith alone. Get Miss Carlyle and Miss Appletree to help you. You may give the child a small dose of laudanum this morning and another tonight. It should help her sleep."

Althea followed his directions and sat with Meredith until the little girl finally drifted into a restless slumber. Miss Appletree tiptoed in, motioning that she would stay with the child, and Althea thankfully slipped from the room. Her back ached from bending over Meredith, and the throbbing in her head had intensified. She desperately needed a few moments of peace and quiet.

Althea sought sanctuary in the blue drawing room. The doors to the garden stood open and a slight breeze stirred the air. She sat down on the sofa, leaned her head back, and wearily shut her eyes. A cup of tea would be delightful, she thought, but had not the energy to get up and pull the bell rope.

Aunt Pysie found her there an hour later. She entered quietly, but Althea heard the door open and sat up. Slightly disoriented, she rubbed at her eyes. "Is Meredith awake?"

"No, dear, she's still asleep," Aunt Pysie said, taking the chair opposite. "I looked in on her just now and she seems to be resting better. Would you like a cup of tea? I would myself, and I asked Mrs. Pennington to bring us a tray here."

"Thank you, it is just what I need. Do my ears deceive me or has that infernal racket finally ceased?"

"The workers are having a bite to eat," Aunt Pysie said, smiling. "Dreadful, the noise they set up. One can hardly hear one's self think."

Mrs. Pennington arrived with the tea and arranged the tray between them. Althea was content to sit still and allow Aunt Pysie to prepare her a cup. She accepted the tea and sipped it thankfully, her head starting to clear. It was a moment or two before she became aware that Aunt Pysie was unnaturally quiet and moving restlessly in her chair.

"Is anything wrong?" she asked, alarmed. "Meredith is not worse?"

"No, no, my dear. Meredith is fine, as I told you.

I was just thinking, Althea, and there is something I wish to discuss with you. Have you given any further thought to what Andrew said last night?"

"His announcement? No ... not really," she hedged. There was no point in mentioning the sleepless night she'd endured.

"I think he means to announce his engagement at the ball," Aunt Pysie declared in a rush. "That is why he wants the ballroom restored. It is all part of the tradition."

"It is possible, I suppose, but ... to whom?"

"He has not said anything to you then? I had hoped, that is ... well, if it is not to be, it is not to be," she finished in her rambling fashion.

Althea rubbed her head. "What is not to be?"

"Oh, it has all come to nothing, and doubtless you will think me stupid, but I *had* hoped Andrew would have the good sense to offer for you. Then we could all go on quite comfortably."

Althea hid behind her teacup. She was loathe to admit that she, too, had entertained the same notion and the thought of it had kept her awake the entire night. Keswick had been very attentive to her. Sometimes she fancied there was a new warmth in his eyes when he regarded her, but perhaps it was merely wishful thinking on her part.

Certainly her feelings for him had undergone a change, and she cherished Perry Demont's words to her. But Althea knew she was not sophisticated like Louise or meek and dutiful like her cousin. She thought Keswick had mellowed. He was no longer the sort of autocrat he'd been with Deborah, but Althea still argued with him. She could never be the kind of wife who would unthinkingly accept his word as law. Yet she could think of several occasions when he'd yielded to her wishes, and even Aunt Pysie had remarked on his thoughtfulness. Like having Deborah's portrait painted as a surprise. Surely that indicated a degree of caring beyond what he might be expected to feel for his wife's cousin, did it not? But if he intended to make an announcement at the ball, he would have most assuredly said *something*.

"Of course I know the idea is ridiculous," Aunt Pysie was saying. "It is only that I am so fond of you. And if he does not mean to marry you, then I must make plans because I do not think I can live here with anyone else." The words ended on a sob and she drew out her handkerchief.

"Aunt Pysie," Althea cried, moving to kneel beside the older woman. "How can you say such a thing? Why, the manor is your home, and no matter who Keswick weds, I am certain she would be delighted to have you here."

"No, I am not so much of a fool as to believe that," she said, dabbing at her eyes. "I mean well. You know I do, Althea, but I do foolish things. I cannot help it. Only look at the mess I made with Eugenia Yardley's specific."

"A mistake that could have happened to anyone, dearest, and there was no harm done."

Aunt Pysie sniffed. "The entire house reeked. Although that is not as bad as when I caught the curtains in here on fire. If you had not been so quick, Thea, the house might have burned to the ground."

"You are exaggerating, Aunt Pysie. Besides, those curtains were so hideous they deserved to be burned. Even Keswick has said the room looks much better in rose."

"But you did not tell him why we changed it, which is exactly like you. You never say a word when I do something silly, or talk too much, and you never make me feel uncomfortable like Lady Penhallow or Lady Fielding. I could *never* live with them."

"As they are both already married, Keswick cannot offer for either of them, so you need not worry," Althea teased, hoping to coax a smile from her.

"But he will offer for someone just like them, Althea, and I shall be in the way here. They will make me feel old and useless and . . . and I cannot bear it."

"Dearest, you are making too much of this. Anyone who comes to know you must love you as I do."

That produced a tearful smile and Aunt Pysie wiped at her eyes. "I was hoping you would say that, Thea, because I want to come and live with you. No, dear, let me finish. It is improper of me to say so, but I love you more dearly than either of my nephews. You are like a daughter to me and I know we could live comfortably together. I have an independence—Andrew makes me a very generous allowance—so I could share the expense of a cottage. We could lease a small place, perhaps near here, so we could still see Meredith."

Althea, deeply touched by the hopeful, pleading look in Aunt Pysie's eyes, felt herself close to tears. She kissed the older woman on the cheek. "I think it is a splendid idea."

With all the problems besetting her, Althea was much inclined to remain at home instead of attending Lady Fielding's ball. She was extremely tired and although her headache had eased, it had not entirely departed. She also disliked leaving Meredith when the girl was so ill. When she mentioned the idea to Keswick, however, he would not hear of it.

"I spoke with Mayhew before he left the house. He thinks Meredith will likely sleep through the night, and you have already exhausted yourself sitting with her today. Allow Miss Appletree to watch over her, and if Meredith should take a turn for the worse, she can send word to us at Lady Fielding's. We can be back here within an hour. You do trust Miss Appletree, do you not?"

"Yes, of course—"

"Then there is no more to be said. Now go and rest. You look tired, Thea, and I do not wish people to think I browbeat you."

"You are browbeating me now, sir," she answered with a weak smile.

"So I am, and if you do not obey me, I shall carry you up the stairs myself." He took a step toward her, and Althea threw up her hands in mock defense.

"I am going, my lord," she protested, and left the room with a backward glance. Keswick stood, hands on hips, grinning at her. She wondered if he would have dared pick her up. Smiling to herself as she went up the stairs, she had an idea he would not hesitate. It would have created quite a scene, she thought, and wondered what it would feel like to be held in his arms. Wicked girl, she scolded herself, but fell asleep dreaming of his embrace.

Mary woke her an hour later so she would have

ample time to dress for the ball. Althea was ready with plenty of time to spare, despite the maid's lengthy ministrations. She wore a deceptively simple white slip covered with a soft blue-gray gauze, and her only adornment was a single strand of pearls. She refused to use any cosmetics and it was only at Mary's insistent pleading that she allowed the maid to weave a white silk ribbon through her curls. Althea draped a soft blue Kashmir shawl across her shoulders, picked up a small blue and ivory silk fan, and declared herself ready. Begging Mary not to wait up for her, she walked down the hall to check on Meredith one last time.

Althea opened the door to the child's room quietly, not wishing to disturb Meredith if she was sleeping. In the soft glow of candlelight she saw Keswick bend over his daughter's bed and brush her brow with a light kiss. Having no wish to intrude on such an intimate moment, she softly shut the door and hurried down the stairs. Aunt Pysie was waiting for her in the great hall.

Keswick joined them a few moments later, lavishly complimenting both ladies on their attire. He looked very handsome, as Aunt Pysie told him, in a dark blue double-breasted tailcoat, white waistcoat, and light blue pantaloons. Bowing, he offered each lady an arm. "I shall no doubt be the envy of every gentleman in Cumberland when I walk in with two beauties," he teased.

Aunt Pysie tapped him lightly with her fan for such nonsense but smiled happily at Cheever as he held the door for them. Althea remembered the last occasion when they had driven out together and prayed Lady Fielding's ball would prove a more enjoyable evening.

At least they managed to arrive at Graystones, a dignified stone house of moderate size, without incident. Lanterns hung from the trees to light the drive and the windows blazed with candlelight. It was a beautifully warm night and the windows were all raised. Hearing the laughter floating down to them, Althea began to anticipate a pleasant evening.

Keswick assisted his ladies from the carriage, through the house, and up the broad stairs. Lady Fielding and her daughters stood at the top of the steps to receive them. Edith appeared to be enjoying her role as hostess while Lizzie fidgeted, anxious to join the guests congregating in the ballroom.

Lady Fielding welcomed them with genuine warmth and, in answer to Keswick's inquiry, explained that Sir Edward was in the library. "It is the gout again. I fear it is worse than usual and it pains him to stand for more than a few moments."

"Oh, the poor man," Aunt Pysie said, quick to sympathize. "And how vexing for you. If I had only succeeded with the Yardley Specific we would have him right as a trivet in no time."

"The Yardley Specific—" Lady Fielding began, and was interrupted as both Althea and Keswick hastened to speak.

"If you ladies will excuse me, I shall just look in on Sir Edward," Keswick said before retreating to the first floor.

"Come along, Aunt Pysie," Althea urged the older woman. "We must not monopolize Lady Fielding and I see Lucinda Deerborn waiting for us."

Althea guided the older woman into the brilliantly lit ballroom. Many of the guests had already arrived. They promenaded the length of the room in small groups while the musicians tuned their instruments. Lucinda, looking unusually flushed, was the first to greet them. She praised both ladies on their becoming gowns before whispering to Althea, "Wait until you see Captain Hewlett's friend."

George Selwyn approached before she could say more. "Ladies, you are all looking particularly fetching this evening."

"Thank you, George dear," Aunt Pysie said, stretching up to kiss his cheek. "It is kind of you to include me when I know you mean Althea and Lucy. Now you and the girls run along. I mean to sit with Lady Penhallow for a spell."

George obliged her by offering an arm to each of the young ladies and steering them in the direction of the lower end of the ballroom. Althea heard a delicate laugh ring out. She recognized the sound even before she turned her head and glimpsed Regina Montague. The slender blonde was gazing admiringly at a very tall, very elegant young gentleman. Since Captain Hewlett stood beside the man, Althea assumed this must be his friend. A quick glance at Lucinda confirmed her guess, for she was looking daggers at Miss Montague.

Captain Hewlett caught sight of them and hailed George. "Here, Selwyn, this is grossly unfair. You should not be permitted to stroll about with two lovely ladies while Lord Prescott and I must vie between us for the favors of one."

"It is your penalty, sir, for deserting us for the

charms of London," Lucinda teased. Her pointed look at Regina gave the words a barbed edge.

"Hardly a penalty, Miss Deerborn," Regina shot back. "Not when you consider the far superior attractions of London."

The gentlemen shifted uncomfortably and Althea tried to smooth over the situation. " 'To every thing there is a season, and a time to every purpose.' And that includes London," she said sweetly, giving her hand to the captain.

He bowed and placed a chaste salute on her gloved hand. "Miss Underwood, it is indeed delightful to see you again. Was that quotation from Shakespeare? Or Byron, perhaps?"

"Neither, sir," she said, endeavoring not to laugh. "It is from Ecclesiastes."

"Don't believe I know the fellow," Hewlett remarked, his brow creased in thought. His friend coughed discreetly, reminding the captain of his presence. "Oh, may I have leave to present Lord Prescott?"

"No need to introduce me to Miss Underwood," the gentleman said, stepping forward. "I met her in London several years ago, though I doubt she recalls the occasion."

Althea studied him, the combination of green eyes and blond hair seeming vaguely familiar, but she had not been in London for the better part of six years and the memory eluded her.

"Lawrence Tremayne at your service, Miss Underwood," the gentleman prompted, executing a neat bow. His green eyes held a hint of laughter.

"Mr. Tremayne? Is it really you?" Althea cried, delight shining in her eyes as she extended her hand.

146

"Never tell me you know this rag-mannered ruffian," the captain said. "How comes this about?"

"You have not forgotten then?" Prescott asked.

Conscious of everyone's regard, Althea withdrew her hand but bestowed a warm smile on the gentleman. "No, indeed. I do not forget gentlemen who have done me a signal service." She turned to the others. "Lord Prescott rescued me in London. I was foolish enough to be caught walking when a sudden storm blew up. He put his carriage at my disposal and I fear he took a dreadful soaking as a consequence."

"It would seem to be a habit of yours," Regina murmured.

If Althea heard her, she gave no sign of it. "I never had the opportunity to properly thank you, sir. I heard you left London rather suddenly."

"To my regret," he said, nodding. "My uncle died unexpectedly and as his heir I was needed at home. By the time I returned to town, *you* had left London."

"Mind your manners, Miss Underwood," Hewlett teased. "Tremayne is Viscount Prescott now and a toplofty fellow if ever there was one. All puffed up with his own consequence."

"Yes, and I shall pull rank on you and demand the first dance with Miss Underwood . . . that is, if she will grant me the privilege?"

Althea agreed, blushing slightly under the scrutiny of his green eyes. She gave him her dance card and watched him pencil in his name opposite the opening minuet. He hesitated for a fraction of a second before putting his name beside a quadrille later in the evening.

George intercepted the card as Prescott started

147

to return it and wrote his own name down for a country dance. Captain Hewlett and Prescott solicited Regina and Lucinda to stand up with them. Similar scenes were being enacted the length of the ballroom as young couples met and dance cards were filled. Voices lifted in conversation and the sounds of excited laughter could be heard above the muted stirrings of the instruments.

The pleasurable buzz of camaraderie died suddenly, a hush settling over the room. Lord Filmore entered and paused just inside the door. He was of a height to be easily seen over the heads of most of the guests, and his black coat and pantaloons set him at odds with the rest of the gentlemen. He stood proudly, gray eyes raking the room.

No one moved or spoke for the space of a moment. Then a rush of conversation filled the air.

"Who is that magnificent creature?" Regina demanded. "He reminds me of a panther ready to strike."

Someone answered her, but Althea did not hear it. She watched Filmore stroll across the room. He spoke briefly with one or two matrons before Richard Kingsly stepped rudely in front of him. The younger man, easily a head shorter, placed a hand on Filmore's arm and spoke insistently. His emphatic gestures and unsmiling countenance indicated an anger that left Althea feeling uneasy. Filmore brushed off Kingsly's arm and turned his back on the man while he was still speaking.

The direct cut was an insult. Althea had a premonition there would be trouble over it before the night was done. She felt a measure of relief when Edith Fielding hurried forward and linked her arm in Richard Kingsly's, leading him from the floor with more tact than one would have given the girl credit for. Her sister, Lizzie, was equally quick to intercept Jack Filmore. She held tightly to his arm, forcing him to slow his steps. Althea watched as they moved inexorably toward her.

Prescott's voice sounded softly in her ear. "If I may be of service, Miss Underwood, you have only to give me the nod."

Althea turned. Lord Prescott's large frame was a reassuring presence. She was glad she'd promised him the first set. Surely the musicians would begin the opening chords at any moment.

"Filmore, old fellow," Hewlett said over her shoulder. "Glad to see you home again and thank you for bringing Lizzie to me. She's given me the honor of leading her out for the minuet."

Lord Filmore acknowledged the greeting and transferred Lizzie's hand to the captain. He spoke to George briefly and shook hands with Lord Prescott before turning to Althea. The opening strains of the minuet started and couples were edging forward to form their sets. Filmore looked down at her. There was something in his eyes, almost a pleading look, which touched her deeply.

"This is my dance, I believe," Prescott said before Filmore could speak, breaking the tension between them.

Althea allowed him to lead her out onto the floor, but she felt a pang of sympathy for Filmore. She need not have worried. He asked Lucinda to stand up with him and her friend accepted with every appearance of delight. George was duty-bound to ask Miss Montague. He did so, but with such poor grace he expected to be rebuffed. Regina accepted him, much to his surprise, although neither looked pleased at the prospect as they took their places.

The dance seemed interminably long to Althea. She was pleased to see Prescott again, and he danced with a smooth elegance that gave him an air of London sophistication. She was aware that they were the cynosure of many eyes and normally would have enjoyed the attention. The problem was Jack Filmore. She was much too aware of his presence, and too concerned with Keswick's reaction, to enjoy the minuet. Her eyes kept straying to the door. Keswick was bound to return to the ballroom at any minute.

The last strains of the music signaled the end of the set. Althea rose from a deep curtsy and heard the spectators applauding lightly. Prescott gave her his arm as they left the floor. He spoke so quietly, only she could hear his words.

"Forgive my presumption, Miss Underwood, but for all you dance divinely, I fancy you are unusually agitated. Is it something to do with Lord Filmore? I do not mean to pry, but if I can be of any use to you, you need only say the word."

Althea glanced up at him in surprise. Was her concern so transparent then? She made an effort to smile. "Thank you, my lord. You are most kind, but if you truly mean to do me a service, I pray you will ask some of the young ladies present to stand up with you. Otherwise they shall all regard me with envy."

He laughed. "As you will, Miss Underwood. I shall not intrude further on your affairs."

Lucinda glided up beside her, her escort in tow. "Althea dearest, you looked wonderful dancing. In fact, if you were not my dearest friend, I would likely scratch your eyes out. Even Lord Filmore could not keep his eyes off you."

"You exaggerate, Lucy, as ever you did," Filmore scolded her while his eyes scanned the room.

"I think not, sir, and I suggest we trade partners." Lucinda grinned impudently at Prescott.

He returned her smile but glanced questioningly at Althea. She nodded and he moved off with Lucinda as the opening notes of a waltz sounded.

"Shall we?" Filmore asked, extending his hand. Althea moved into his arms. He was as tall as Keswick but leaner. She felt the strength of the man as his hand exerted a gentle pressure on her back. She followed him easily and they half circled the room before he spoke.

"I believe I owe you an apology, Miss Underwood. I was unforgivably rude when we last spoke."

"If you were, I quite deserved it for presuming to speak to you of personal matters." She expected him to utter some sort of denial, and when he did not, she glanced up at him.

"Why did you?" he asked. It might have been a rebuke, but he was smiling and his eyes did not look so harsh in the candlelight.

Althea did him the courtesy of considering her reply before she answered. "It was an impulse, my lord. I know something of how you must feel, but perhaps it would be better if we did not discuss this in the middle of a ballroom."

"You are correct, of course. Even now everyone is wondering what I can have said to make you look so grave. Can you bear to smile at me?"

She did so willingly, and he swept her into a series of turns that made the candles seem to tilt alarmingly. When the tempo slowed, he looked down at her. "Will you meet me tomorrow? In the same place?"

Althea hesitated.

"I know it is a great deal to ask, but I would like to talk to you about my brother. I . . . There is no one else I can speak about Oliver with, no one who would understand."

It was wrong of her to meet him secretly, but she sensed a need in him to talk. She remembered how she'd felt when Deborah died, and her compassion was stirred anew. They could not discuss such matters if he called formally or if she rode out with him chaperoned. "It will have to be early, my lord," she warned. "Ten o'clock?"

He agreed and seemed to relax as he maneuvered her expertly down the room. Althea turned in a graceful swirl of blue gauze and her gaze encountered Richard Kingsly. She missed a step and felt Jack Filmore's arm tighten as he steadied her. Kingsly, his shoulders hunched forward and arms folded across his chest, stood slouched against the wall glaring at Filmore's back.

Althea looked up at her partner. "Whatever did you say to young Kingsly? He looks positively furious."

Filmore glanced around. "That insufferable puppy? He had the infernal gall to criticize Keswick to me. I merely put him in his place."

"Oh, of course, my lord. How incredibly foolish of the man to approach you, of all people, to vent his hatred of Keswick." She watched Filmore's face as her words registered. For an instant he

152

looked startled and she held her breath. Then a slow smile appeared, softening the harsh lines of his mouth.

"You are a worthy adversary, Miss Underwood. I see I shall have to be careful crossing swords with you. As for Kingsly . . ." He broke off, tilting his head in a gesture of contempt. "My quarrel with Keswick precedes his. He shall have to wait his turn." Filmore's smile disappeared abruptly. He gave her no chance to say more but swept her in a final turn, ending the waltz with a flourish.

Althea found herself released suddenly, Filmore's hand dropping from her own as though his fingers burned. His face was inscrutable, the gray eyes like pieces of flint. She knew without looking that Keswick stood behind her. Had Filmore deliberately positioned them to end their waltz in front of him?

She prayed silently for composure as she turned. She knew everyone was watching, most hoping for a scene. Althea laid her hand lightly on Keswick's sleeve, but she doubted he was aware of her presence. The two men stared at each other in stony silence.

Regina Montague broke the tension. Pulling George along with her, she pushed through the crowd until she reached Keswick and tapped him on the arm with her fan.

"La, sir, it is past time you put in an appearance, but you need not fear. I contrived to save you the next quadrille and a waltz, although I vow you do not deserve it."

Keswick glanced down at the girl, seemingly puzzled. Then he smiled at her. "How very kind of you, Miss Montague. I shall certainly look forward to waltzing with you, but I am engaged to Miss Underwood for the quadrille." Althea's hand still rested on his right arm and, without looking, Keswick covered it with his left hand, holding her tightly by his side.

Regina flinched as though she'd been struck.

George patted her arm, chuckling aloud as though it were all a good joke. "No point in arguing, Miss Montague. My cousin is accustomed to doing as he pleases and taking whatever he desires. Just ask Filmore here. Is that not right, Jack?"

Filmore deliberately ignored George and bowed slightly to Regina. "I should be honored if you would accept me as a substitute for Keswick. I may not be as accomplished on the dance floor, but I can promise not to tread on your slippers."

Regina turned a haughty shoulder to Keswick and batted her eyelashes at Filmore. "In truth, my lord, I would much prefer *your* company," she said, loudly enough for them all to hear, before she walked off on Filmore's arm.

"If you will excuse us, George?" Keswick said politely, stepping around his cousin. Althea looked back at George as they took the floor. He looked alone, rather forlorn, but she had scant time to feel sorry for him. Keswick demanded her attention.

"What the devil do you mean by allowing Filmore to lead you out? Can I not leave you alone for more than a few moments without you creating a scene for everyone in the county to gossip over?"

"I beg your pardon, my lord, but it was you who created a scene, not I," she shot back in a low

154

voice. "I see no reason why I should refuse to stand up with Lord Filmore merely because you dislike him."

"You are mistaken, Thea," Keswick said more quietly, a strain of unbearable sadness running behind his words. "It is Filmore who despises me." His lips pressed together in a bitter line and the liveliness seemed to drain from his eyes. "Heed what I say, my dear. I do not want you near Jack Filmore. At least not until we know for certain who is behind the attack on me."

Chapter 9

The clang of hammers woke Althea at an early hour. Unable to go back to sleep, she rose and was nearly dressed by the time Mary appeared with her morning chocolate. Althea finished buttoning the jacket of her riding habit, only half listening as the maid gently scolded her.

"Miss Althea, you should have rung for me. I would've been up here before this, but I thought you'd be sleeping late this morning seeing as 'ow you didn't get home till close on three."

"Thank you, Mary, but as you can see I am quite capable of dressing myself." She paused to sip the chocolate. "I appreciate your concern, but I do wish you would not wait up on my account. I have told you a dozen times that I do not need such cosseting."

"Yes, miss," the maid replied, stepping behind Althea to adjust the fall of her jacket and smooth the lines of the riding skirt. "Miss Appletree said I was to tell you Lady Meredith has been asking for you. Poor little soul cried her heart out last night when she woke and found you was gone, but she looks fair to mending this morning."

Althea smiled. "Thank heavens! I am relieved to hear she is better. I did hate leaving her. She is so rarely sick that she does not understand when she must be confined to bed. I vow she is the worst patient in the world."

"No worse than her papa," Mary said, chortling as she handed Althea the green hat that matched her habit. "Look 'ow he behaved when the doctor ordered him to stay off that foot."

"Yes, they are much alike, are they not? Well, run along, Mary, and please tell Miss Appletree I shall look in on Meredith directly."

"Yes, miss. Should I send Frank to the stables and have your horse brought around?"

"No, do not!"

Mary paused at the door, looking back at her curiously.

Althea realized she'd spoken too quickly. "I really do not know how long I shall be with Meredith," she hastened to explain. "I'll go to the stables myself when I am ready."

When Mary left without further argument, Althea closed her eyes, breathing a sigh of relief. She was not made of the stuff of heroines. The necessity of keeping her tryst with Filmore a secret preyed on her nerves. She did not believe she was doing anything wrong, but she felt guilty all the same.

She opened her door moments later and was startled by a loud, piercing cry. *Meredith!*

Althea ran down the hall only to draw back as she neared the door to Meredith's room. Keswick's unmistakable voice, raised in laughter, warned her that he was within. Meredith's high-pitched giggles followed. She certainly was not hurt. Quickly, Althea ducked into Miss Appletree's room and stood just inside the partially opened door.

She did not want to face Keswick this morning, not when she intended to deliberately disobey him. Althea waited an agonizing ten minutes, her heart racing wildly. What on earth could she say to Miss Appletree if the governess found her lurking there? At last Althea heard Keswick's voice in the hall. Holding her breath, she waited several more minutes before cautiously peering out the door. There was no sign of him and she slipped quickly into Meredith's room.

"Aunt Thea, Aunt Thea," Meredith cried, bouncing exuberantly on the bed. "Papa says I can get up today."

"Your papa said *maybe*, Lady Meredith," the governess corrected. "And only if you rest quietly this morning."

Althea leaned over to hug Meredith, kissing her lightly on the brow. "I am very glad to see you looking so much better, darling. Now, are you not glad I sent for Dr. Mayhew? You shall have to thank him the next time you see him."

"I will," she promised. She tugged at Althea's arm, trying to pull her down on the bed. "I want you to sit with me. Read me a story, please, Aunt Thea?"

"When I come back from my ride," Althea promised.

"I want to go, too," Meredith announced, half climbing out of the bed before Althea caught her by the elbow.

"You lie down here and behave yourself. Remember you promised your papa you would rest this morning."

Meredith wrinkled her nose and scrunched her lips in a pout. Althea lifted her crop in a mock threat, but the effect was spoiled by Buttons. The puppy jumped on the bed, barking excitedly as he leaped at the riding crop. His yelps mingled with Meredith's shrieks of excitement. Althea pretended to back away in terror and then rushed for the hall. Miss Appletree followed her retreat and the two women spoke briefly before Meredith's plaintive cries compelled the governess to return.

Assured the child's fever was broken, Althea left her with a lighter heart. She hesitated for an instant, then chose to leave by the back stairs. Better an encounter with one of the servants than Keswick. If he knew she planned to ride this morning, he just might decide to join her.

She paused outside the stables. Assuring herself that Keswick was nowhere in sight, Althea summoned enough courage to take the few steps inside. Mason stood a dozen feet away, his back to her, conferring with a stable lad. Jeremy must have mentioned her presence, for Mason turned almost at once and hurried to her side.

"Miss Underwood, no one told me you was riding today. Do you want your mare? She's feeling her oats and a run would do her good."

"The mare will do fine, Mason, thank you." She watched him snap his fingers at the lad and Jeremy scurry toward a stall.

"We'll have her ready in just a moment, miss," he promised. "We're a mite behind this morning. Lord Keswick's been in here grilling Jeremy about Grimsby. Did he tell you the news?"

"Not yet. We missed each other at breakfast. Have you found out something then?" She was pleased her voice sounded casual. Let Mason think the earl would tell her the news, though she very much doubted it. He had some misguided notion of protecting her from this business.

"Well, Jeremy went over to Cockermouth last week. His ma lives there and she's been feeling right poorly, so I gave him leave. Anyways, he goes into town for his ma and who does he see but Grimsby strolling out of the Castle Inn just as big as life. Jeremy pretended like he didn't see him and hotfooted it back here. We told his lordship first thing. He's driving over there this morning."

"Is Jeremy certain it was Grimsby he saw?"

"Dead sure, Miss Underwood," Mason said, and hailed the lad as he brought out her bay mare. "His lordship questioned him backwards and forwards and is convinced it's our lad."

"Perhaps I should wait then—"

"Now don't you be thinking of going with his lordship 'cause you know he won't allow it. 'Sides, like as not, it'll be a waste of time. I'd be more than a mite surprised if Grimbsy's still there. Stands to reason, miss. If Jeremy saw the lad, then Grimsby must have seen him, too. Now, if you was Grimsby, would you be awaiting around for his lordship to pay you a visit?"

Althea smiled and accepted the leg up Mason offered her. The groom made sense, but more to the point she knew it was highly doubtful Keswick would permit her to accompany him. She thanked the groom and turned the mare out of the yard.

Mason had been right about her mount. The little gray was impatient to run and Althea had her hands full holding the horse to a canter. It was too dangerous to gallop on the road, but the mare tried her best. However, Althea's hands remained firm on the reins and the horse finally settled to a steady gait, leaving her free to concentrate on Lord Filmore.

Could he possibly have planned the attack on Keswick? Althea tried to consider the matter dispassionately. Her instincts told her it was unlikely, but Keswick obviously had doubts and he knew the gentleman far better than she did.

She glanced over her shoulder and spotted the groom, young Johns, riding at a discreet distance. His presence was reassuring. Keswick would be furious enough if he learned she'd met with Filmore despite his warnings, but doubly so if she went unchaperoned. The groom provided her a modicum of propriety—and protection.

Keswick obviously thought she needed the protection. She recalled his anger when he'd led her out on the dance floor. He had explained it away as concern for her safety, warning her to steer clear of Filmore until they learned who was responsible for cutting the saddle girth. It made sense, she supposed, but she could not help wondering if Keswick's anger had been aroused, at least in some measure, by jealousy. Last night he had behaved as though he truly cared, showering her with attention and seeing to her every want. She remembered the intimate way he'd held her in his arms when they'd danced, the tenderness of his gaze . . . She shook her head. Perhaps it was only wishful thinking on her part.

She reached the meadow and leaned forward, patting the horse's neck. "Okay, girl, let's go." The mare's stride lengthened instantly as she broke into a gallop and the grass flew by beneath her feet. The rush of air helped to blow the disturbing thoughts from Althea's mind, and the warmth of the sun lifted her spirits. She gradually tightened the reins to slow her mount as they neared the woods on the far side. It was just going on ten o'clock. Would Filmore be waiting?

Althea dismounted and led the mare down the dirt path to the clearing. She saw Filmore at once. He was sitting on the large boulder where they had talked the day before. Hearing her approach, he waved and slid off the boulder with the agility of a mountain cat.

Althea turned her back. Suddenly nervous, she busied herself tying the mare's reins to a willow tree.

"I wondered if you would come, Miss Underwood," Filmore said, his voice directly behind her.

She spun around, knocking against him. Filmore reached out an arm to steady her, but Althea stepped hastily back.

Filmore dropped his arm at once, his gray eyes dark as flint. "Having second thoughts, Miss Underwood? Or have I turned into an ogre overnight? I assure you I would not have asked you to meet me had I known you would be frightened. Perhaps you'll tell me just what it is you fear?"

"Why, nothing, my lord. You merely startled me."

His brows arched in disbelief. "I did not invite you here to ravish you, if that is what you are thinking."

Althea laughed, an unconvincing trill that did more to betray her nervous state than a scream would have done. She saw the hurt in his eyes and cursed her own foolishness.

"I am sorry to have troubled you. Good day, Miss Underwood," Filmore said curtly, turning toward his own mount.

"Wait!"

He glanced back, his mouth set in grim lines and his eyes cold.

"I apologize, my lord," she said softly. She took a step forward and held out her hand. "I own I am uncommonly nervous, but it is not because I fear you. May we start anew?"

He studied her in silence for a long moment, but her eyes met his unwaveringly and he finally accepted her hand. "You relieve me greatly, Miss Underwood. Do you care for a seat in the sun? Or shall we remain here in the shade?"

"The sun, please." She allowed him to escort her to the large boulder. Neither spoke, but it was not an uncomfortable silence. Althea waited patiently.

Filmore sat with one knee drawn up, his arm resting across it. He stared out at the water and did not look at her when he finally spoke. "I have thought a great deal about what you said. I only wish I could resolve my feelings as easily as you, but it is not such a simple matter. Did you know my brother?"

"I met him once or twice. He seemed a pleasant young man."

"He was. Everyone who knew him liked him immensely. He was game for anything. Oliver rode the fastest horses, took the highest jumps, handled his cattle well, and wagered recklessly. Too recklessly." Filmore paused, his gray eyes meeting hers levelly. "He was home on a repairing lease. Keswick knew it. Oliver told us both he had to retrench— he'd backed too many losers at Ascot."

"Your brother obviously had a fondness for gambling that he could ill afford," she said gently. "It was unfortunate—"

163

"Keswick should not have gambled with him. He knew Oliver was up against it and still he sat down with him at the card table."

"Would you have had him insult your brother instead? Only consider if Keswick had not invited Oliver or refused to play cards with him. My knowledge of a gentleman's code of conduct is scant, I admit, but I fancy your brother would not have accepted such behavior lightly."

"You defend him well, but even if, as you say, Keswick was forced to sit down with Oliver, he did not have to take everything from him."

She laid a hand on his arm. "I truly do not believe Keswick had a choice. Your brother insisted on wagering his fortune on one turn of the cards. He'd had too much to drink and would not listen to reason. Keswick judged it wiser to allow the bet and planned to return Oliver's vowels later."

"So he says."

"I was there that evening. I heard the altercation and came out into the hall."

Filmore turned away and sat without speaking for several moments. He brought one hand up and rubbed it back and forth across his brow. It was a troubled gesture and Althea wished there was something she could say to comfort him.

"I cannot let go," he said at last. His voice shook, jagged with sorrow.

Prompted by instinct alone and not at all sure of what she was urging, she whispered, "You must."

"I cannot," he moaned, cradling his head against his arms. "Hating Keswick keeps Oliver alive for me. It is all I have left." The words were muffled, barely audible.

"What will you do then if Keswick dies?" Althea

asked, her voice deliberately sharp and meant to provoke. The words were a gamble, and she prayed she was right.

Filmore's head came up. He gazed at her as if she had suddenly run mad.

"Someone tried to kill him." Althea uttered the words briskly and they lingered on the air, at odds with that peaceful setting. "Keswick thinks it might have been you."

Filmore continued to stare at her, his eyes probing the depths of her own. "What kind of game are you playing, Miss Underwood?"

"No game, sir, though I wish it were. The girth on Keswick's saddle was deliberately cut. It was only by the merest chance that he took a low jump with it. He sprained his ankle. A higher fence might have broken his neck. The groom who saddled his horse disappeared the same day."

"Good God, I do not—" he began, only to break off his thoughts, shaking his head. Filmore slid off the rock and paced in front of her as though he could not contain his agitation. "You will have to forgive me, but this is incredible. Beyond belief."

Althea observed him closely. Filmore was either totally astonished or a consummate actor. She hoped it was the former. She had one more card to play and said quietly, "Of course it could be just a coincidence that you returned home at the same time."

"Keswick cannot believe I would ever have a hand in anything so despicable."

"Why ever not? *You* have no trouble believing Keswick planned your brother's ruin and deliberately drove him to his death." Her voice sounded remarkably calm to her own ears, but she had difficulty controlling her trembling hands and clasped them tightly together.

"I never said that Oliver's death was deliberate."

Althea slid off the boulder and stood facing him, her head thrown back. "You imply it, sir. You imply it every day you continue to wear mourning. You imply it with your continued hatred of a man who was once your best friend." Her voice shook with the intensity of her words, but she stood perfectly still, holding his eyes with her own. She saw his rage flash briefly, to be replaced by a troubled, confused look. Filmore was the first to turn away. His shoulders bowed, he trudged slowly to his stallion. Althea watched him lead his coal black horse toward the path.

Filmore slowed his steps as he passed her and lifted his head. "Give Keswick a message for me. Tell him he has my word as a gentleman that I had nothing to do with the attack on him."

Althea remained where she was, filled with an overwhelming sense of relief. Whatever Keswick might think, she was convinced of Lord Filmore's innocence.

Mason met Althea as she rode into the stable yard and gave her a hand dismounting. "I'm glad you're back, Miss Underwood. Looks like a storm might be blowing up."

Althea agreed. Dark clouds were gathering and the breeze was stronger now. "You can almost smell the rain, but what are you doing here? I thought you'd be on your way to Cockermouth."

The groom shrugged. "His lordship decided to wait until tomorrow. I take it you didn't see him then? He rode out not long after you."

"Did he?" she asked, a feeling of dread causing her to shiver. "Has he returned yet?"

"Yes, miss. About ten minutes back. Something a-worrying 'im, too, by the looks of 'im. He was right short with Jeremy."

Althea handed over the reins, lost in thought. Had Keswick seen her with Filmore? She had the uncomfortable notion she would know soon enough and her footsteps lagged as she walked to the house. Aunt Pysie met her in the hall.

"I am so glad you are back, dear. I feared you would take a soaking. Is it not odd how the weather turns so unaccountably? I don't mean to second-guess our Lord, but I do think that in a better-ordered world storms would not blow up without warning. Are you chilled? Would you like some tea? You look a bit pale."

"I am fine, Aunt Pysie, thank you, and tea would be lovely. Just let me change first." She started toward the stairs, but Aunt Pysie's words stopped her.

"Andrew was out, too, and came back as cross as a bear, though he was quite cheerful this morning when the sun was shining. Do you think the weather affects some people that way? He was almost rude to Lady Penhallow and I fear she took offense. Poor George, too."

"Somehow I doubt it was the weather," Althea said with a sinking heart. "Where is he?"

"George or Andrew? Andrew took himself off to the ballroom and George has gone. He drove Lady Penhallow back," Aunt Pysie replied, a hint of gloom coloring her voice. "She only came because she wants Eugenia Yardley's journal, you know. Do you think it wrong of me not to give it to her? She

167

says *she* is the proper person to have it, and she tried to make dear George say so, too, but he refused to be drawn into an argument, though he did point out that Eugenia left her journal to me. And even if I did make a muddle of the specific, I might succeed were I to try again." She paused, looking at Althea with hopeful eyes.

"Keep it, darling. Mrs. Yardley meant for you to have it. If you like, I shall help you with the recipes."

Aunt Pysie seemed immensely cheered and Althea hurried up to her room to change into a morning dress. Bows met her at the door and she picked up the kitten, cuddling him for a moment. Keswick *had* seen her. She knew it with a certainty beyond questioning.

"The question is, what does he think?" she asked the kitten, setting him on the bed. Bows tilted his head, silently regarding her with large, round eyes as she donned a morning dress.

"He saw me with Lord Filmore. Will he think I have a fondness for the gentleman and it was a lovers' tryst?" The kitten mewed and licked his paw. "Or ... Oh, Lord! Could he possibly think I am plotting with Filmore against him? No, he would not believe that. Would he?" The kitten mewed again. Althea picked him up and scratched him behind the ears. "Come along, fellow. I may have need of you."

Aunt Pysie was waiting for her in the drawing room. Althea put the kitten down beside her chair. It was cowardly of her, but she intended to have a cup of tea before facing Keswick. She accepted the cup handed her and made an effort to focus her attention on what Pysie was saying. Something about the ballroom.

"You would not credit the number of men in there, my dear. Why, there must be above three score. I declare I never thought there were so many laborers in all of Cumberland."

"I can well believe it, judging by the racket they are producing. How is the work progressing?"

"You have not seen it? It is quite amazing, Thea. I never thought Andrew could have the work done in time, but they are progressing much faster than one would have thought possible. Andrew said he intends to take the old chandelier down later today and have it thoroughly cleaned before they hang it again."

Althea sipped the hot, sweet tea, its warmth reviving her. "I shall have a look in a few moments. I need to talk to Keswick, and I suppose I might as well beard the lion in his den."

"Bear," Aunt Pysie said, biting into a raspberry tart.

Althea looked at her in confusion. "I beg your pardon?"

"Bear," she repeated. "Today he is like a bear with a sore paw. Not a lion, you know, though I suppose to beard a bear in his den does not sound quite right. I wonder why? Perhaps Sir Walter got it wrong and it was a bear he meant, although now that I think of it, it does say in the Bible somewhere that one should not behave like a lion in the house."

"I shall be certain to tell Keswick so, ma'am," Althea said, setting her cup down. "Look after Bows for me."

The pandemonium in the west wing assaulted

her senses as she stepped through the door. There were workmen everywhere, all shouting to be heard above the clamor. It was the first time Althea had seen the ballroom and she gazed around in awe.

The room was vast, its walls soaring upward to a height she could only guess at. The ceiling was the crowning masterpiece with its elaborate scrollwork and heavy oak beams radiating outward from the immense chandelier in the center. Halfway down the walls a narrow balcony circled the room, enclosed by a three-foot-high railing of elaborate wrought iron. On the lower level the north and south walls were broken by a series of tall windows. She could see a crew of gardeners working outside to cut away the heavy ivy covering the panes. It did not require much imagination to visualize how impressive the room would appear when finished.

At present, however, the din was deafening. The noise bounced off the high walls and reverberated through the room. Even if she were able to find Keswick, it would be quite impossible to carry on a conversation. Two carpenters rushed past carrying several long planks. Althea stepped hastily back, narrowly avoiding a collision with a painter. Her foot slipped on the sheeting used to protect the new oak floor. She would have fallen if a strong arm had not reached out to rescue her.

Althea turned, surprised to find Keswick beside her. She looked up, catching an odd expression in his dark eyes. It vanished, replaced by a look so fierce she hesitated to speak.

He didn't waste time trying to make himself heard above the noise but took her arm and pulled her to safety in a small alcove. He motioned for her to wait there and stepped back out into the chaos of the room. She saw him gesture to a large, brawny man, who waved in response. A moment later an ear-piercing whistle sounded above the din. Almost magically, the level of noise lessened to a minuscule level and the laborers began filing from the room. Keswick stood where he was, watching the exodus. When the ballroom was finally cleared, he motioned for Althea to join him.

She crossed the narrow space between them carefully, eyes downcast, wary of the treacherous sheeting. "I am sorry," she said as she reached him. "I did not mean to interrupt the work in here. I had no idea there would be so many people or so much confusion . . ." She stopped, spreading her hands helplessly.

Keswick shrugged. "They would have halted for their midday meal shortly. Why are you here?" His voice was curt, his manner unyielding, and she knew he would not make it easy for her.

"I wished to speak with you. Can you spare me a few moments?"

"I'm listening."

"I saw Lord Filmore this morning," she began, pleased she sounded fairly calm.

He glanced at her then, his dark eyes unfathomable.

When he didn't speak, she rushed on. "I went riding and he was in the clearing on the far side of the meadow." Let him think the meeting was accidental. "I saw no harm in speaking with him. I knew young Johns was keeping an eye on me."

Keswick walked away and seemed intent on examining the freshly applied plaster near the door. "Simmonds is doing an excellent job on this wall."

Althea stayed where she was, nonplussed. "We were discussing Lord Filmore."

"You may have been, but I have no desire to do so," he said, walking a little farther along the wall.

Althea picked up her skirts and followed him. "He asked me to give you a message. He said to tell you that, on his word as a gentleman, he had nothing to do with the attack on you."

Keswick shrugged, his back to her.

"Does that mean nothing to you? I thought you would be pleased." She stood beside him and laid a hand on his arm.

He turned, anger blazing in his eyes. "Pleased? Pleased that you met clandestinely with a man I expressly asked you to avoid?" He seized hold of her arms as though he would shake her. "Do you take me for a fool?"

"At the moment, yes. Please release me. If we cannot discuss this civilly—"

"Civilly? You provoke a man to his limits and then expect him to behave civilly? You picked the wrong man to play games with, my dear Althea. I warn you I will not behave as *civilly* as the others." He loosened his hold on her briefly but only to sweep her into a closer embrace. His lips came down on hers, hard and demanding.

Althea struggled for an instant. Keswick's arms were like iron bars across her back and one hand held her head firmly beneath his. Her own arms were trapped between them and she used her fists to beat ineffectively against him. The tattoo she drummed against his shoulder gradually slowed as she tasted his lips, warm and inviting now. Her fin-

172

gers uncurled and unconsciously crept around his neck as she willingly returned his kisses. She strained her body against his, wanting only to be held as close as possible. The reality was far better than her dreams.

Althea felt his lips leave hers and protested with a soft cry. Her lashes fluttered open and she looked up at him in innocent surrender. The passion reflected in his eyes reassured her. She could have broken the embrace then, but she leaned back comfortably against his arms.

"I've wanted to do that since the first time I saw you," he whispered, a finger tracing the line of her cheek and moving to her lips. Althea kissed the tip of his finger, and he groaned aloud before taking possession of her mouth again.

Sensations swirled through her and she lost herself in the rapture of his embrace. She felt Keswick's lips against her neck and then in the hollow of her throat, spreading a delicious wave of warmth through her body. She clung to him tightly, her knees suddenly weak, her breath coming in rapid gasps. She loved this man and joy flooded through her with the knowledge that she was loved in return.

Keswick lifted his head slightly, kissing her lightly on each eyelid. He waited, and when she opened her eyes, he kissed the tip of her nose before setting her from him. "Little witch, do you wish to drive me over the brink into madness?"

Althea stood still and silent, her hair disheveled, her eyes unnaturally bright, and her skin becomingly flushed. She smiled, an unknowingly seductive smile.

Groaning, Keswick strode away. He needed distance between them or he would take her on the dirty sheets covering the floor. It was difficult to think of anything but his overpowering desire for her. Remembering the way her soft lips had yielded beneath his own inflamed him. His hands ached to caress the sweet curves of her body. Desperately, he looked around in search of a distraction.

"Keswick, come back. We have unfinished business," she called, her voice teasing, almost caressing. She started to follow him.

"Stay where you are," he ordered. "I cannot think clearly with you near me."

"Do not think then," she advised with a laugh, and took a step forward.

He retreated to the center of the room. "If you have a heart in that tempting body, then leave me for a while. I am no saint, Thea."

His voice, raw with passion, echoed around the room, sending a shiver of desire through her. She stood still, enjoying the knowledge that she had some power over him. Had she moved or spoken she might have missed the alien sound that intruded, a creaking noise like the groaning of rafters. She looked up and saw the massive chandelier shift suddenly.

"Keswick!" she screamed, the same second the monstrous thing plummeted downward. It crashed with a horrendous sound of breaking glass and twisting metal.

"Oh, God! No!"

Althea dashed across the room, slipping and sliding on the sheeting. She fell twice but hardly noticed in her anxiety to reach him. All she could see was the pile of jagged metal covering the spot where Keswick had stood. She screamed his name over and over, but there was no answer.

Chapter 10

The thunderous sound of the chandelier crashing brought the workmen on the run, but Althea was the first to reach the earl. She found him sprawled facedown on the far side of the massive pile of tangled metal, his head twisted to one side, his eyes closed. Althea knelt beside him, crying his name as her trembling fingers explored his back and shoulders. There was no sign of an injury—unless it was to his legs, which were imprisoned beneath the chandelier.

The brackets pinned him. Made of cast iron with gilded gold leaf and designed to hold candles, they were V-shaped and tapered to a fine point at the end. The force of the fall impaled the brackets in the floor like spikes. One on either side of Keswick's legs, with a scant inch to spare.

Althea had only one conscious thought, the need to free him from the wreckage. She tugged desperately at the jagged metal rim just above his legs. The foreman reached her a moment later. Simmonds saw the blood on her hands where the ragged edges had sliced through her tender skin. Althea seemed unaware of the cuts until a drop of blood splashed on Keswick's tan pantaloons. She drew back, staring in horror at the crimson stain but unable to avert her eyes.

Simmonds urged her to move out of the way, but Althea continued to sit motionless. He stepped behind her and as gently as possible lifted her to her feet. "He's going to be all right, miss, don't you worry. Just give us a chance to get him free of this mess."

Althea glanced up at the man, seeing him for the first time. She recognized him as the brawny foreman Keswick had signaled when he had dismissed the workers. She swallowed hard. "What . . . what can I do to help?"

Simmonds considered her. He suspected she was near to fainting and would have liked to consign her to the care of the older woman in the main house, but he doubted she would leave the earl. He compromised. "Would you sit by his head, miss, and let me know if he comes around?"

Althea nodded and Simmonds turned away, shouting directions to his crew. His decisiveness, the authority in his voice as he issued orders, reassured her. She sank to her knees by Keswick, cradling his head in her lap. Her fingers smoothed the black curls off his brow while she watched his eyes for some sign of consciousness. It seemed an eternity before Simmonds returned.

"We're ready to try to move him now, miss. Two of my men will lift him while the rest of the crew hoists the chandelier."

Althea nodded, not understanding what he wanted.

"You'll have to move out of the way, miss," he told her gently, extending a hand to help her up.

Althea moved slowly, her body trembling as she

stood. She watched two burly laborers take her place, one on either side of Keswick, and bit her lip to keep from screaming at them to be careful. At a nod from Simmonds the two men lifted him slightly while several others near his legs simultaneously raised the remains of the chandelier. The two men began to edge slowly backward.

A loud cheer went up as Keswick's boots drew clear of the wreckage and Simmonds motioned the men to halt. "I don't want to move him too far until the doc has seen him."

Althea barely heard him as she knelt beside Keswick again, pulling the sheeting spread about them into a cushion to pillow his head. She was rewarded for her efforts when his eyes slowly opened. It was only for the space of a heartbeat. He closed them again, moaning softly, but it was enough to send her heart soaring. *He was alive.*

Keswick stirred slightly, groaning aloud, and Althea gripped his hand tightly.

"Be still," she whispered, leaning over him. "You must not move just yet. Dr. Mayhew is on his way."

He opened his eyes again to see Althea's tear-streaked face bending over him. A drop of moisture fell on his cheek. "Trying to drown me, Thea?" he managed to murmur before falling unconscious again.

She choked back a sob, praying the doctor would arrive, but even as her mind formed the thought, Dr. Mayhew came striding across the room. He greeted her curtly, then stooped to examine Keswick. Althea waited anxiously while he made a cursory examination, hardly aware that she was holding her breath.

"He'll do," Mayhew announced after a few moments. "A few bruises, but not even a broken bone." He glanced at what remained of the chandelier. "And that's a bloody miracle."

"Are you certain, Dr. Mayhew? Why is he still unconscious? He opened his eyes, but it was only for a second."

"I can't say for sure, but my guess is that that thing hit him in the back with enough force to knock him out. Which is just as well. Leave him, child. He'll come around soon enough, but I prefer to move him while he's still unconscious. More comfortable for him that way. You go ahead and prepare that big drawing room again. Warn his aunt, too."

Althea was prepared to argue. She didn't want to leave Keswick—not for a single moment.

"I beg you will not make things more difficult for me than they already are, Miss Underwood," Mayhew chastised, reading the determination in her eyes. "I depend on you to behave sensibly, and Miss Carlyle will have need of you. Cheever told me she fainted when she heard what had happened. See to her, please."

"But he—"

"He will be fine," Mayhew promised her as he came around to assist her to her feet. He kept her arm in his as he turned her in the direction of the door. "Have that butler of yours get the brandy out. We'll have need of it before we're done, and order tea, if you will."

Althea nodded and took a shaky step toward the door. She turned back for one last look at Keswick, but Mayhew blocked her path.

"Hurry, Miss Underwood. We'll be bringing him through in a few minutes."

179

She started across the room, the distance seemingly vast and the room tilting at an odd angle. She closed her eyes. *I must not faint. I cannot faint. Keswick might need me.* Althea blinked rapidly and some of the dizziness passed. She took a few more steps and Cheever materialized.

"Miss Underwood, if you will allow me?" He placed a firm hand beneath her arm and she leaned thankfully against him.

"The staff is dreadfully concerned, miss. They're saying his lordship was beneath the chandelier when it crashed. Miss Carlyle fainted when she heard." The butler did his best to keep his voice neutral, but he had seen the mangled chandelier and the earl's body lying deathly still beyond it.

"Keswick will be fine," she managed to say, and felt surprisingly better for saying the words aloud. "He will be fine," she repeated, her voice a little stronger. "Dr. Mayhew promised. You will have to ready the south drawing room. They are . . . are going to carry him there." She paused, trying to remember what else the doctor had wanted. "Brandy. The doctor said to have brandy and tea ready."

"I'll see to it, Miss Underwood," he assured her as they reached the hall. Several of the servants were huddled near the door, waiting fretfully for news of his lordship. Cheever informed them briefly that Lord Keswick was not seriously injured and recommended rather tartly that they go about their business. The footmen and the maids scattered, pleased with the news and anxious to spread the word. All except for Mary.

She stood where she was, exclaiming aloud over the state of her mistress. Cheever relinquished

Althea into her care before taking himself off down the hall.

"You come along with me, Miss Althea, and we'll get you fixed up. Why, there's blood all over your gown."

Althea glanced down, vaguely surprised. "It does not matter, Mary. I must be in the drawing room. Keswick will need me."

"Not looking like that, he won't. Lord have mercy, Miss Althea, one look at you and you'll be scaring him out of ten years' growth and Miss Pysie like as not would swoon again. You come along with me. There'll be plenty of time to tend to his lordship."

Although Althea chafed at the delay, it was barely twenty minutes before Mary had her looking presentable again. She'd not allowed the maid time to properly dress her hair, but it was neatly brushed and gathered with a ribbon at her neck. The bloodstained morning dress had been exchanged for a crisp blue-and-white striped muslin that Mary declared most becoming, though Althea did not notice. Mary had also gently cleansed her hands, managing to massage in a soothing balm before Althea finally protested and refused any further ministrations.

She rushed downstairs but checked at the door of the drawing room, unable to believe her eyes. Keswick had been carried there, of course, and reclined on the long sofa—looking remarkably well while arguing with Dr. Mayhew. Cheever stood near the window talking quietly with the brawny man who seemed to be in charge of the laborers. Her eyes traveled back to Keswick. He saw her and gestured at once.

"Althea, come in and save me from this saw-bones. He wants to bleed me merely because I passed out for a few minutes."

"It was more than a few minutes, my lord," she said, crossing the room to stand near him. She studied his features hungrily, but when his eyes met hers with a special tenderness, she looked away, suddenly shy of him.

"Whatever," he said, watching her closely. "I suffered no serious harm save for the large bruise on my shoulder and time will take care of that."

"I still think you should be cupped," Mayhew argued, packing his bag. "However, I will not insist if you'll agree to stay off your feet for a few days."

Keswick grinned audaciously. "I shall agree to rest today, but I make no promises for tomorrow."

Mayhew looked around. "Where is that brandy I ordered?"

Cheever coughed and stepped forward. "I placed the decanter and glasses over here, sir."

"Are you prescribing brandy for me?" Keswick asked as the doctor crossed the room. "Excellent! Just what I would have ordered."

"Not for you, my lord," Mayhew said, pouring a stiff shot. "You will take tea today and like it, or I shall wash my hands of you. The brandy is for me."

Keswick chuckled and watched the doctor drain his glass. "I won't argue with you today, Mayhew—I'm thankful enough to be alive to put up even with your crotchets."

"See how that head of yours feels in the morning. If you have any pain, send for me at once. Ah, here comes your aunt. At least there is one member of your family I can depend on to behave sensibly. Miss Carlyle, how are you feeling?"

Aunt Pysie entered the drawing room, leaning heavily on George Selwyn's arm. She looked shaken and rather wan, but she managed to smile at the doctor. "Much better, sir, thank you. I am certain I shall recover quickly now that I know dear Andrew is not in any danger."

George helped her to a chair near the sofa and moved the table with the tea service nearer her hand. "I think we shall all do better for a cup of tea." He looked across at his cousin. "A close call, Andrew. I understand the old chandelier missed you by inches. You'd best leave the renovations to the workmen."

"Thank you for the advice, George, but my luck seems to be holding, at least as long as I have Althea by me." He glanced at her with a warm smile. "If you had not screamed when you did—"

"Oh, let us not speak of that," Aunt Pysie said with a shudder. "It does not bear thinking of. Althea, sit down, dearest, and you, too, George. Will you join us, Doctor?"

Althea took a chair beside Aunt Pysie, wishing Keswick would not look at her so intimately—at least not in front of his cousin. George would be furious when he learned she was in love with Keswick. She avoided looking at either of them, focusing her attention on the doctor.

Mayhew was shaking his head. "Thank you, Miss Carlyle, but I'll just check on Lady Meredith before I take my leave."

"I'll show him up," Cheever said, leading the way from the room. Mayhew set his glass down reluctantly and followed the butler.

"Guess I'll be going, too," Simmonds said, feeling

uncomfortable in the drawing room. He nodded to Keswick. "Glad you're all right, sir."

"Will you not stay and have a cup of tea, Mr. . . . ?" Althea asked.

"Simmonds."

"Mr. Simmonds. I have not thanked you properly for all you did."

"No thanks are necessary, miss. I just wish I knew what caused the chandelier to fall. I was certain I'd rigged it up safely. If you'll excuse me, I want to take another look up there." He nodded to the ladies and left the room in the doctor's wake.

"I was just saying the other evening—was I not, Andrew?—that the ballroom was dangerous. I hope you do not mean to go back in there. Let Mr. Simmonds oversee the work."

"We shall see," Keswick said evasively. "George, be a good fellow and bring the brandy decanter over here. I think we could all use a splash in the tea."

"Absolutely not," Althea objected. "Did you not hear what Dr. Mayhew said? Nothing stronger than tea for you."

"Really, I cannot think it would be at all wise, Andrew. George, pay him no mind. The tea is quite reviving as it is. I feel much better myself. Althea dear, your cup is almost empty. Shall I refill it for you?"

"Thank you," she answered, holding out her cup. She could feel the warmth of Keswick's gaze on her and searched her mind frantically for a diverting topic. She spoke of the first thing that came to mind. "George, how is it you are here? Aunt Pysie said you called this morning with Lady Penhallow but that you had left to drive her home."

"I did and listened to a thundering scold for my pains. I came back only to offer my apologies to Aunt Pysie. I would never have mentioned Mrs. Yardley's blasted journal if I had known Lady Penhallow would react so violently. The woman was in a positive fury and insisted I drive her over here." He looked contritely at his aunt. "I hope you'll forgive me for bringing her down on your head."

"Of course, George. I confess I have been wondering if I should not give her the journal after all. I fear she will make life dreadfully uncomfortable for all of us, which is surprising for I'd no notion she possessed such an envious nature."

"Why not copy the recipes for her, Aunt Pysie?" Althea suggested. "Then you will both have a copy and Lady Penhallow will have no cause to complain."

"Althea! Why, that is a splendid idea. Now why did I not think of that? I shall begin at once."

"Tomorrow will do," Althea said, smiling. "You have had a very trying day and I think you would do well to rest. We all would," she added with a meaningful look at Keswick.

"I shall take my leave then," George said, rising abruptly. He had seen the look that passed between his cousin and Althea. Jealousy flared in his eyes for a moment, but he quickly composed himself and even spoke warmly to Keswick. "Andrew, old man, do have a care. I should hate to lose you."

"Do not worry, cousin. I am like a cat with nine lives."

"Well, you've already lost several of them, so be careful. If you need assistance tomorrow, consider me at your service. Ladies, do not trouble to show me out. I know the way."

As soon as the door closed behind George, Althea rounded on Keswick. "Now, sir, tell me truthfully how you are feeling. Is your head troubling you?"

"Witch," he mouthed silently, wondering how she had guessed. "It is only a slight headache. I am coddling myself, lying here when there is so much to be done."

"Do not think of moving off that sofa, Keswick, or I promise you, I shall send for Dr. Mayhew."

"Andrew, you must indeed rest. A blow to the head can be very dangerous. Remember what happened to your great-uncle Joseph—" Aunt Pysie stopped, distracted, as the butler appeared at the door. "Yes, Cheever, what is it?"

"Begging your pardon, ma'am, but Mr. Simmonds is wishful of a word with his lordship."

"Bring him in then," Keswick ordered before either of the ladies could protest.

Simmonds appeared a moment later, with one of the gardeners in tow. He nodded to Althea and Aunt Pysie but addressed the earl. "There's something I think you should know, sir. Perhaps the ladies will excuse us?"

Althea would not agree. "Anything that concerns his lordship concerns us all. Let us hear what you have to say."

The foreman looked at Keswick, who shrugged helplessly. "Go ahead, Simmonds."

"Well, sir, like I said, I inspected that chandelier myself before the work ever started. There's a trapdoor in the ceiling that opens up on the third floor in kind of a closet. You operate the chain to lower the chandelier from up there whenever it needs to be cleaned or the candles changed. That chain was solid, sir. I checked every inch of it myself and there wasn't a weak link in the line. If it wouldn't have been so much in our way, I would've taken it down then, only it takes half a dozen men to move the thing and where would we have put it?'"

"Relax, Simmonds. I am not blaming you," Keswick assured him.

"That's not it, your lordship. The thing is, I went back up there after I left you and had a look around. There's about a dozen links connecting the chandelier to the chain. They form sort of a circle around the center and . . . well, here, see for yourself." He extended his hand in Keswick's direction with the palm open.

"What is it?" Althea asked, rising.

Simmonds looked at her as Keswick took the links from his hand. His voice was full of anger. "Eight links out of the chain, Miss Underwood. They were forced open and were still just hanging at the top. Someone rigged that chandelier to fall."

Aunt Pysie fainted, her cup dropping from her lifeless fingers and smashing against the floor. Althea hurried to her side, lifting the older woman to a sitting position on the sofa. "We shall need the smelling salts," she told Keswick.

"Leave her for a moment, Thea. I believe there's more and it might be better if Aunt Pysie did not hear it." He looked at Simmonds, a question in his eyes.

"Yes, sir," the man answered. "Before I came to you with this, I talked to some of my men. Most of 'em had gone home for a bite to eat, but Jim Davies—he's one of the carpenters—was out in the yard cutting some wood strips when the chandelier crashed. Jim says he saw a man running from the house. He couldn't see his face clearly, but for what it's worth, he was dressed all in black."

Althea felt faint herself. "No, no . . . it cannot be." Not Filmore, she thought.

"I wouldn't want you to take just my word for it or my man's," Simmonds told the earl. "So I talked to your gardeners, too. They were working on the north side cutting the ivy away from the windows." He gestured to the man behind him.

Keswick recognized the man. Searching his mind, he came up with the name. "Jarvis, is it? Did you see this man?"

The gardener, a small, wiry fellow, stepped forward nervously, twisting his cap in his hands. "Yes, sir, although I didn't think much about it at the time. Not till Mr. Simmonds mentioned a man all in black. I thought it was just Lord Filmore I saw, a-ridin' that black stallion of his up on the north ridge."

"I see," Keswick said, swinging his legs to the floor. "Thank you, Simmonds, for coming to me. It may already be too late, but if you can keep your men from gossiping, I would appreciate it. I don't want word spread that this was anything other than an accident." Simmonds nodded and Keswick turned to his gardener. "Jarvis, do you understand?"

"Yes, your lordship. I won't be saying nothing."

"Thank you. You may go now. Simmonds, would you find Cheever on your way out and ask him to come in here?"

Keswick waited impatiently, his eyes on Althea. She was sitting beside his aunt, rubbing Aunt

Pysie's hands. She kept her back turned to him, and the silence lengthened.

"Althea." The word was a command.

She glanced around, tears in her eyes. "I must see to Aunt Pysie," she murmured, her voice strained.

He started to approach her, but Cheever hurried in, smelling salts in his hand.

"Mr. Simmonds told me Miss Carlyle had fainted again," he said by way of explanation. He handed the bottle to Althea and watched as she waved it beneath Aunt Pysie's nose. After a moment the older woman's eyes fluttered open and she moaned softly.

Althea stood. "Will you help me take her up to her bedchamber, Cheever? I believe she should rest for a while."

The butler nodded and grasped Aunt Pysie by one arm while Althea took the other. Barely conscious, Aunt Pysie's eyes focused on Althea with a plea for help. "I . . . I do not understand . . ."

"Come along, darling. We will take you upstairs and you can lie down for a while. Try not to worry about anything, Aunt Pysie. We will talk later." They were almost to the door when Keswick spoke.

"Althea?"

"I shall be back as soon as I can, my lord."

It was, in fact, almost an hour before she returned and Keswick had used the time well. As soon as she entered the drawing room, Althea noticed the brandy decanter was now on the tea table, almost empty. She smelled the fumes as she sat down opposite him. Keswick reclined on the sofa, his head thrown back against the cushions, his

189

eyes closed. She thought at first that he was asleep and started to rise again. His voice halted her.

"I thought you meant to avoid me, Thea." He opened his eyes, gazing at her reproachfully.

"Aunt Pysie is seriously disturbed. I finally gave the poor dear a dose of laudanum to calm her. I only hope she may sleep for a while." She reached for her cup, though of course the tea was now cold.

"Try the brandy," Keswick advised, watching her.

"I see you have—in spite of Dr. Mayhew's warning." Her words were not meant as a rebuke. She was too weary for that, but Keswick seemed to take offense.

"I think a drink or two was warranted, my dear. Would you not agree, in light of the fact that my old friend Jack tried to murder me?"

"I *cannot* believe it of him," Althea said, resting her head against the back of the chair. She closed her eyes as exhaustion swept over her. "It could not have been Filmore. He told me his hatred of you is all that keeps his brother's memory alive. If you died, so would his brother."

"I see. Apparently, you had quite a little chat this morning," Keswick drawled.

"We did," she owned with a sigh, too much on edge to think clearly, too tired to consider the effect her words might have. She opened her eyes and passed a hand across her brow. "It is really very sad. I believe I am the first person he has ever spoken with about Oliver's death. Grief is tearing him apart, Keswick. He told me how you were such close friends as boys. I think he is walking a thin line between hating and loving you."

"And he confided all of this to you?" Keswick asked, his tone incredulous. He continued with biting sarcasm, "It seems a rather intimate conversation to have with someone whom you just happened to meet accidentally."

"What are you implying, Keswick?" she asked quietly.

He looked down, apparently intent on examining the damage to a cuff on his shirt. His voice, when he spoke, was elaborately casual. "I should think it obvious, my dear. How long have you two been meeting?" He gazed at her then, his eyes cold and pitch-black. "I'll wager my life this morning was not the first time."

A guilty blush betrayed her. Recalling her first meeting with Filmore, she could not honestly deny his accusation.

"I suppose your silence answers me." He swung his legs to the floor and reached for the brandy.

"I met him accidentally yesterday and we talked briefly," Althea tried to explain as she felt the tears rising behind her eyes. "Then last night, at Lady Fielding's ball, he asked me to meet him to talk about Oliver. He thought I would understand because of . . ."

"Because of Deborah?" Keswick said, finishing the sentence for her. "I see. I am to be cast as the villain in this little drama. The pair of you must have had a wonderful time carving me up. Of course your sympathy would be all for Jack, and never mind that he tried to kill me."

"You are being ridiculous, sir! Either the fall or the brandy has disordered your senses. I *told* you I had seen Filmore this morning. Do you think I would have done so if we were having some sort of tryst?"

"I think you told me because you knew I had

seen you," he snapped. "Did Mason tell you I was out riding? Is that why you rushed to the ballroom to find me?"

It was too near the truth. Althea looked down at her hands. It was a moment before she finally answered him. "Believe what you will about me, Keswick, but you are a fool if you think Lord Filmore had anything to do with these attacks on you."

"Come, Althea, do not let your partiality for the man blind you to the facts. Who else dresses entirely in black and rides a black stallion? Are you so besotted with him you cannot think rationally?"

"Rationally? You are the one who is incapable of rational thought. Why, anyone could have dressed in black and ridden a black horse. It could even have been Kingsly. The color does not belong to Lord Filmore exclusively."

"How sweetly you leap to his defense, Thea. Almost passionately, one might say."

She stared at him, unable to believe what she was hearing. Keswick sprawled on the sofa, brandy glass in hand. Except for the bitter edge to his voice, he seemed totally indifferent to her. What had happened to the tenderness he'd shown her earlier? Had she only imagined the love in his eyes? There certainly was no sign of it now. The tears she had barely managed to check filled her eyes. She shook her head in a helpless gesture as she stood. "I cannot talk to you now."

He grabbed her hand as she swept past him. "Wait, Althea. Can you not see that I am only trying to make you realize how dangerous Filmore can be—"

"Let me go," she cried through her tears. Wrenching her hand free, she half ran across the room.

Cursing loudly as the door closed behind her, Keswick hurled his glass at the wall.

Chapter 11

Althea, confused and exhausted by her emotions, requested Mary to bring a dinner tray to her room. The chef took care to prepare a particularly enticing meal, but for all his effort she barely touched the food. Too restless to retire yet unable to face Keswick, she left her room to look in on Meredith and Aunt Pysie.

The little girl appeared to be her own exuberant self once more. Althea was thankful, but Meredith's enthusiasm and liveliness grated on her nerves, exacerbating her headache. She left the child to the tender mercy of Miss Appletree and retreated to the relative calm of Aunt Pysie's bedchamber.

Althea glanced about as she entered and could almost smile at the disarray. The room was like Aunt Pysie, charming and disorganized. Papers and magazines covered every available surface. Large bolts of material for wall hangings completely hid one of the wing chairs. Needlework projects, begun with zeal and later abandoned, were strewn about haphazardly. Three large vases overflowed with freshly cut roses, filling the room with their heavy scent.

In the midst of it all Aunt Pysie lay nestled under the covers of her massive canopied bed. She, too, had dined in her room and the remains of her dinner could be seen on the small round table placed conveniently to her right.

"Dearest, do come in," Aunt Pysie called weakly. Sitting up in bed, surrounded by a half-dozen pillows, she stretched out a hand. "Tell me what the world is coming to, Thea, for I vow I sometimes think I am losing my mind."

Pushing several pillows out of the way, Althea sat down gingerly on the edge of the bed. She grasped the older woman's hand, studying her pale features. "How are you feeling, Aunt Pysie?"

"Dazed. I have thought and thought of what that man said until my head aches and still I cannot conceive of anyone wishing to harm Andrew. Could he have been mistaken? Could it not have been just an accident?" she asked hopefully.

Althea shook her head. "I am afraid not, darling, but you must try not to worry. Let Keswick deal with this."

Aunt Pysie's gnarled fingers trembled in Althea's hand and tears seeped from the corners of her eyes. She looked around the room as though she no longer recognized her surroundings. "It was a wicked, evil, evil thing to do and I know the Bible says we must forgive our enemies, but I *cannot*. Would you send someone for the vicar? I should like to talk to him this evening."

"Perhaps you should wait until tomorrow," Althea suggested, searching for words to reassure her. She was alarmed to see Aunt Pysie so distraught, for the older woman had a naturally optimistic nature and usually managed to see some ray of hope in even the direst of circumstances. Althea squeezed her hand. "I know you are overset. It is quite understandable, but, dearest, remember problems always seem bleakest at night. In the morning we shall be able to think more calmly."

"The morning will not alter what has happened," Aunt Pysie said, her chin quivering.

Althea released her hand, moving closer to hug her. Aunt Pysie sobbed against her shoulder and Althea thought it best to let her cry. She held her, patting the older woman's back and making soothing sounds while she listened to her disjointed mutterings.

"It is so shameful," Aunt Pysie cried repeatedly. "I cannot bear it. The evil of it. Shameful. What would his mother say? Oh, dear Lord, give me strength."

Fearing Aunt Pysie was growing hysterical, Althea eased her back on the pillows. "Rest a moment, dearest," she told her, and hurried around the bed to find the laudanum amid the jumble on the other table. With shaking hands she prepared a dose and persuaded Aunt Pysie to swallow it, while wondering if she should send for Dr. Mayhew. She had never seen Aunt Pysie so distraught.

Althea sat on the bed and spoke inanely of anything that came to mind, anything but Keswick. She told her how Meredith was progressing and all the things the child wished to do. At last, when Aunt Pysie's head began to nod, Althea eased the pillows from behind her and covered her with a warm quilt. She stood for a moment, watching her. Aunt Pysie's breathing had slowed and she appeared to be resting comfortably.

Althea hesitated and then pulled the bell rope. When Mary arrived, she explained her concern about Aunt Pysie. "Would you have a cot moved in here and stay with her tonight, Mary?"

"Of course, Miss Althea. Don't you be frettin'. I'll watch over the old dear. I expect the accident to his lordship was too much for her nerves. A bit of a shock, like."

"Call me at once if she wakes," Althea cautioned.

"I will, so put your mind at rest. You should be in bed yourself, miss, if you don't mind my saying so. You're looking awfully tired."

That was nothing compared to how she felt, Althea thought. She returned to her own room and slowly prepared for bed. There was only a numbness inside of her now. Was it just this morning she had felt such incredible joy? She'd put all thoughts of Deborah aside and succumbed to Keswick's kisses. Willingly. She'd admitted she loved him and thought she was loved in return. And now?

She had no answers for herself. She did not know if Keswick truly cared for her. There was a strong attraction between them certainly. She blushed, recalling their kisses and her own mounting desire. She'd been drawn to Keswick since the first time they'd met—the day he'd married her cousin. Althea was ashamed to admit that even then she'd found Keswick undeniably attractive and had often been impatient with Deborah for her fear of the man.

The night Keswick left the manor house to go abroad, Althea had spoken with him alone in the library. He'd asked to see her privately to discuss the provisions he'd made for Deborah while he was away. Keswick had been furious, but Althea had thought his anger a mask. She'd suspected he was hurt by Deborah and still grieving over Oliver's suicide.

She had stood close to him, their heads bent together over the account books. She'd tried to make sense of the long columns of numbers but found Keswick's nearness too distracting. All she'd wanted was to comfort him, to ease the pain from his troubled eyes and tease back the insolent grin to his lips. But of course that was impossible, and she'd forced herself to concentrate on the accounts. When they'd finished, Althea had given Keswick her hand in farewell, begging him to have a care while he was away.

"You think me a poor excuse for a husband, I suppose?" he'd asked.

"No, just poorly suited to Deborah," she'd replied, and smiled up at him. "Were I married to you, my lord, you would dance to a different tune. I would not tolerate your rages."

Keswick had returned her smile, but a hint of regret had darkened his eyes and been reflected in his voice. "Have I been so bad, Thea?"

"Not . . . not entirely," she'd answered, shaken by the sudden intensity of his gaze.

"I am sorry for the row the other night. I should not take my temper out on you."

"Better me than Deborah."

"It would have been better had I wed someone more like you . . . Well, my dear Thea, this is farewell. Try not to think too harshly of me."

Keswick had bent his head just as Althea had glanced up. For an instant she had thought he meant to kiss her lips, and for another instant she had shamefully longed for him to do so. His mouth, however, had lightly grazed her brow and then he had been striding out the door and out of her life.

It had been five years since that night, but Althea was no nearer to understanding her feelings or Keswick's. She sighed, blew out the candle, and climbed into bed. Closing her eyes was a futile effort; sleep would be a long time in coming. Was Keswick having difficulty sleeping? Or was he lying awake, thinking of her? Wishful thinking again, she thought. More likely, he was considering the attempts on his life.

Althea, despite the evidence, could not believe Filmore was responsible. He had seemed genuinely shocked when she told him about the cut saddle girth. Could he have spoken as he had and then, less than an hour later, tried to murder his old friend? And would he have been foolish enough to carry out such an attempt wearing his distinctive black clothes?

She'd felt an immediate rapport with Filmore, had known instinctively that they could become good friends. Could she feel that way about a man evil enough to commit murder? Unbidden, the thought came to mind that whoever the guilty person was, it was someone she knew, and knew well. Someone who knew the house. A chilling notion.

She tried to clear her mind of such troubling thoughts. Tomorrow would be soon enough to deal with everything. Tomorrow she would sort out her feelings. She closed her eyes and then opened them again, feeling lonely and bereft. Her kitten jumped up on the bed and padded his way across to her pillow. He mewed softly, rubbing his cold nose against her cheek. She reached an arm up to cuddle him close, comforted a little by his warm presence.

* * *

Althea slept the deep sleep of exhaustion, her tired body finally shutting down her mind. Her first concern when she awoke was for Aunt Pysie, who, Mary assured her, was feeling somewhat better although she was still asking to see Mr. Goodall, the vicar. A footman had been dispatched to ask the gentleman to call.

Althea nodded and then, rather casually, inquired, "How is his lordship this morning?"

"As cross as all get-out." Mary grinned, assisting Althea into her riding habit. "Evans says you'd be taking your life in your hands to gainsay him this morning. It 'pears like he drowned his pain in a couple bottles of brandy last night and his head's paying the toll. Mayhap by the time he returns he'll be feeling more the thing."

"Returns? Where did he go?" Althea whirled about, her distress plainly showing.

"Now don't be frettin' yourself, Miss Althea. Mason's with him. From what Evans said, his lordship wanted to see some gentleman over in Cockermouth."

"And no one tried to stop him?" she demanded, furious that he would risk his life so foolishly. "Dr. Mayhew said he should rest for several days."

"I wouldn't try telling that to his lordship. Evans did and got a boot thrown at his head for his trouble."

Althea dismissed her maid, needing some time to compose herself. Concern for Keswick battled against her anger at the man's irresponsible behavior. She fumed as she adjusted her riding hat. Keswick was impossible and she hoped his carriage hit every rut in the road to Cockermouth. She hoped his head would ache unbearably. She picked up her riding crop and started down the stairs, fear for Keswick tying her stomach in knots. Obstinate, stubborn man, she thought, and prayed he would return home safely.

She left word for Aunt Pysie that she would return shortly and headed for the stables. Young Johns was in charge and his agitation on seeing her was apparent. She eased his mind considerably when she asked that her mare be saddled, then added, "And your own, too. You might as well ride with me."

Althea chatted with Johns about horses and the weather while they rode, but her mind was preoccupied. Still, she was no nearer to finding an answer to her problems when they reached the crest of the hill an hour later. Johns spotted the two riders in the distance first and gestured to Althea. She knew the black stallion at once, but even with her hand held over her eyes to shade the sun, she did not recognize the other rider until they were within hailing distance. Lucinda.

She waved, turning her mare in their direction. Lucinda's cheerful voice beckoned her.

"Althea! How wonderful to meet you this way. I was just telling Jack we should ride across the meadow and pay you a call," her friend said, laughing at Filmore's obvious discomfort. She seemed to glow with good health. The morning sun had painted a blush on her cheeks and the breeze stirred her hair. She looked altogether delighted with life.

Althea smiled at her, noting the use of Filmore's given name, and managed to greet that gentleman with a measure of calm that belied the turmoil in her stomach. He, too, seemed unusually cheerful, although he still wore his customary black.

"If you do not object, I shall ride with you a ways," Althea said, nudging her mare. Johns dropped back a discreet distance. "I am glad I chanced to meet you here, Lucy. This morning would not be a good time to pay a visit. Aunt Pysie is in bed, poor dear, and Keswick has ridden over to Cockermouth, despite Dr. Mayhew's orders that he should rest." She glanced at Filmore. He looked neither surprised nor unduly alarmed. In truth, she thought his attention more centered on Lucinda than on her own conversation.

"My word," Lucinda said, "it sounds as though you have had quite a morning. What ails Miss Carlyle? Should I ask Mama to call with some fruit or something?"

"No, but thank you. She will no doubt be fine in a day or two. Her nerves are overwrought and she's worried about Keswick. He was overseeing the renovations of the ballroom yesterday when the chandelier fell, narrowly missing him."

She had Filmore's attention now. He stared at her, a question in his gray eyes.

"Gracious! Keswick was not hurt, was he?" Lucinda asked. "You mentioned Dr. Mayhew."

"He was just stunned, I believe, though he was unconscious for quite some time and his legs were pinned beneath the chandelier. He does not seem to have broken any bones, but the doctor did want him to rest today. The whole thing upset Aunt Pysie dreadfully, of course."

"Small wonder. You must have had your hands full with the pair of them."

"Excuse me, Miss Underwood," Filmore interrupted, "but did they determine what caused the chandelier to fall?"

"I believe Keswick has some notion," she replied evasively. "He was not best pleased by the knowledge."

"I should think not," Lucinda declared. "Why, he might have been killed. Well, I always said he leads a charmed life. Now, Althea, I do hope he will be feeling more the thing in a few days, and Miss Carlyle too, for I want you all to come to a dinner Mama is planning. It will probably be set for Friday." She dimpled and gave Filmore a mischievous look. "Jack will be there, of course."

Althea looked from one to the other with the uncomfortable feeling that she was intruding. "It sounds wonderful, but much will depend on Aunt Pysie. I had best return to her now. I dislike leaving her alone for very long."

Neither protested as she turned her horse. Glancing back at the pair, Althea doubted either of them missed her very much. All she had learned for her pains was that Lucinda apparently harbored a *tendre* for Filmore, and if the indulgent looks he'd bestowed on her were any indication, a match was well in the making.

Was a man in the midst of courting a young lady like Lucinda apt to be contemplating murder at the same time? Althea didn't think so, but if not Filmore, then who? Richard Kingsly? He *had* been furious with Filmore at the ball. Was he capable of devising a plan to kill Keswick, implicating Filmore at the same time? It was possible, she thought, but admitted to herself that she only favored Kingsly as a culprit because she did not particularly care for the man.

"It looks like a storm might be rising, Miss Underwood," Johns said, breaking into her thoughts.

Althea scanned the dark clouds and agreed. "Let us not waste time then," she called as she booted the mare and sent her racing across the meadow. Young Johns had a hard time keeping up with her. They beat the rain by a matter of moments, and Mason met them in the stable yard.

"I'll take the mare, miss. You'd best hurry to the house before you get caught in the storm. His lordship was asking for you."

"Is he all right then, Mason?" she asked as she dismounted and handed him the reins.

"He didn't come to no harm, if that's what you're asking, but he's not in very good spirits, miss, not by a long shot."

"I see. Well, did you find out anything about Grimsby in Cockermouth?"

"No, miss. Just like I suspected. He's long gone, but I'll let his lordship tell you about that."

Dodging the falling raindrops, Althea made her way to the house. The sun had disappeared and the gray day perfectly matched her mood. Questioning Keswick was not at the top of the list of things she would most like to do. She would have to speak to him sooner or later, however, and now might be a good time.

Cheever opened the door for her and informed her that Keswick was in the south drawing room. She briefly considered changing her attire before approaching him but owned it was only a delaying tactic. *He* would not object to riding dress.

Althea marched resolutely down the hall. She squared her shoulders and lifted her chin before tapping on the door. Keswick's deep voice gave her leave to enter, though his tone was not what one would describe as welcoming. Nor was he resting, as he should have been, but was standing near the windows. He turned when she entered, and she thought he looked almost glad to see her.

"Good afternoon, Keswick. How are you feeling?" Althea was pleased her words sounded calm and rather serene. Quite remarkable really when her insides were twisting around in a distressing manner and the palms of her hands were damp.

"Well enough," he replied tersely. He remained where he was, surveying her coolly from head to toe. "I see you have been out riding. Another meeting with Filmore perhaps?"

"As a matter of fact, yes," she answered, ignoring his sarcasm and seating herself in the wing chair. "He was out riding with Lucy and I chanced upon them. I learned nothing to the point, however."

"How unfortunate," he muttered, turning his back to her. "You might have done better with him alone."

"There is that, of course, but he and Lucy looked to be inseparable. They invited us to a dinner her mama is giving on Friday. Naturally I said we would have to let them know ... but I suspect an announcement will be made then."

Keswick slowly turned, his eyes full of questions, but Althea would not say any more. She had already said too much. The rest was up to him. She looked down at the riding crop in her hands and waited.

She heard a smothered curse and knew a moment of utter despair before she heard Mrs. Pennington's voice at the door. "Cheever told me you were back, miss, so I went ahead and brought you tea. Turned nasty outside, it has. A nice cup of hot tea will set you right."

"Thank you, Mrs. Pennington," she said, managing to mask her exasperation as she smiled at the housekeeper. "Keswick? Will you join me?"

He nodded, crossing the room to the sofa as Mrs. Pennington took herself off. Althea thought he looked less angry . . . Or was it only her imagination? She wished he would say something. Anything.

"I drove over to Cockermouth this morning," he finally remarked, taking the chair opposite her.

It wasn't what she wished to hear, but it was a start. "So Mason said. I gather our pigeon has flown the coop?"

"From what we could learn, he left the same day Jeremy spotted him. Thank you," he added as she handed him the cup, their hands touching briefly. "It was not a complete loss, however."

"Was it not?" she asked confusedly. The touch of his fingers filled her with unbearable longing and she glanced at him hungrily. It was odd that she'd never noticed how one of his eyebrows arched slightly higher than the other.

"If you continue to stare at me like that, Thea, I warn you I shall not be responsible for the consequences."

It was hardly a threat, not when his words warmed her all over and his voice made a caress of her name.

"Do you want to hear about Grimsby or not?"

Not, her heart voted. Her head behaved more sensibly, at least it did once she looked away from his mesmerizing eyes. "Of course I do," she managed to say, and dutifully stared at her own cup. Perhaps then she could concentrate on his words.

"Grimsby met a pretty little barmaid at the inn where he was staying. The teasing wench had every man in the place battling for her favors. In exchange for a few pieces of silver, she told me all I wanted to know. Grimsby wants her to elope with him. He promised her he'd be coming into some money and anything she wanted was hers. She is to meet him in Penrith on the fifth of the month, which happens to be tomorrow. He apparently had business matters to settle first. I fancy he will be rather surprised when I show up in her place."

"Surprised and dangerous," Althea warned. "Keswick, you will not go alone?"

"I think that might be best. If I arrive with Mason and Jeremy in tow and he sees us, he is liable to bolt again. Alone, I stand a chance of persuading him to talk with me. I doubt the boy is dangerous, and he will relax when he knows I do not mean to prosecute him. It is the man who paid him that I want."

"If you will not take Mason, at least allow me to go with you. Surely Grimsby would not be frightened by my presence."

"Absolutely not! I don't want you anywhere near the man. It would be entirely too dangerous."

"You just said it was not—"

"Not for me. But it would be if I had to worry about you. Althea, promise me you will stay in the house until I return tomorrow, and not a word about this to anyone."

"Do you still suspect Filmore then?" she asked, a trace of sadness lacing her words.

Keswick hesitated, choosing his words carefully.

"I think if Jack wanted me dead, he would call me out and be done with it. He was never a coward. But I don't rule him out entirely. He has been obsessed with his brother's death and that can do strange things to a man. Let us just say that I would be surprised if it turns out Filmore was behind this."

Aunt Pysie tapped on the door and poked her head in. "Oh, you are both here! Thank heavens." She bestowed a weak smile on the pair of them and crossed the room to sink heavily onto the sofa. "Mrs. Pennington told me you'd returned, Thea dear, and I am glad to see you and Andrew together. I do think families should be united in times of crises. The vicar said so, too. He said I should take comfort in the pair of you."

There did not seem to be anything to say to that, and Althea offered her tea instead, thinking that for all her cheerfulness Aunt Pysie still looked pale and drawn. Her hands trembled slightly as she took the cup from Althea.

"Are you feeling quite the thing, Aunt Pysie? Perhaps you should have stayed in bed today. I could come up and sit with you."

"No, this is much better," Aunt Pysie said, settling her bulk more comfortably and favoring Keswick with a fond glance. "Andrew, dearest boy, you have been blessed all your life, but you must not feel guilty over it. It is the lump of clay thing, you know."

He choked on his tea, then glared at his aunt indignantly. " 'Lump of clay'? I have, on occasion, been described as many things, but never, dear Aunt, as a lump of clay."

"Now, do not take offense, Andrew. You are a

fine-looking man and I did not mean to infer else. It is only what Mr. Goodall said, though he cannot take the credit, for he read it aloud from the Bible. Romans, I believe. You are the honorable vessel. Quite a comforting thought, really."

Keswick did not look the least bit comforted, and Althea, judging it wise to divert the conversation, inquired instead about Mrs. Yardley's journal. Aunt Pysie was not at all averse to discussing the various remedies mentioned, and aside from a few derisive comments from Keswick, the rest of the afternoon passed peacefully.

Miss Appletree brought Lady Meredith down to join them at four and both Buttons and Bows were allowed in the drawing room. It was warm and cozy inside. The heavy rain pounding against the windows promised to keep the world and its troubles at bay. For a time Althea was able to forget the attempts on Keswick's life. Even Aunt Pysie looked better. There was more color in her face, and she chuckled aloud when Bows suddenly dived from Althea's lap, landing on the back of the sleeping puppy.

The storm cleared before dinner was over and Althea took advantage of it, saying she wished to get a breath of fresh air in the gardens. Aunt Pysie merely cautioned her not to remain too long in the dampness and retired to her rooms, while Miss Appletree bore a sleepy Meredith off to bed. It would have been a perfect time to tackle Keswick, but he had locked himself in the office with Mr. Reading, his overseer, claiming pressing concerns. Althea suspected he was deliberately avoiding a discussion of his trip to Penrith on the morrow. He had mentioned it briefly at dinner, when Aunt Pysie had asked about his plans. Very casual he had been, knowing full well she could not argue about it in front of his aunt and Meredith.

Well, he was not going to have everything his own way. Not if she had anything to say about it. Not even if she had to follow him on her own, though she hoped that would not be necessary. There would be little she could do by herself if someone attacked him. That was why she had sent the note to George. If he was at home, and she fervently prayed that he was, he should have received her summons by now. She could expect him anytime within the hour.

Althea wished she'd brought a wrap out with her. The dampness made her feel chilled and she briskly rubbed her arms. She could not risk going back inside for a shawl. If she missed George, he would be admitted by Cheever and Keswick would know. She had no doubt he'd guess what she intended and somehow put a stop to it. She broke off a rose, managing to prick her finger, and her agitation increased. Perhaps George was away from home.

Althea had decided to give him another five minutes when she heard the sound of a carriage and hastened to the drive. She called softly to George, although with the estate office at the rear of the house, it was extremely unlikely that Keswick would hear them.

"Althea? What on earth are you doing out here?" George demanded, climbing down from his carriage. His tiger ran to the horse's head while he crossed the gravel to where she waited.

"I wanted to speak with you privately. Keep your voice down, please. If Keswick finds out—"

"What the devil's amiss? If he has done anything to harm you—"

"Of course he has not! Pray do not be foolish, George."

"Your note said you required my help urgently. What else was I to think?" he muttered sulkily. His tone was not at all encouraging.

Althea strained to see his face, but the night was cloudy and she could barely make out his features. Still, he was her only hope. She laid a hand on his arm, pleading softly, "George, I really need your help. Keswick plans to drive to Penrith tomorrow. The whole story is too long and involved to discuss now, but I believe he may be in danger. If you could meet me here in the morning, we could follow him and be on hand in case . . . well, in case Keswick has need of us."

"Have your wits gone begging, Althea? What kind of danger could he possibly be in that he could not handle himself? Keswick would not thank you for interfering in his affairs, you know, or me either."

She saw there was nothing for it but to tell him the whole and quickly explained that the chandelier falling had not been an accident. "And it is not the first time he was attacked," she added. "He took a fall a few weeks ago when we were out riding. His saddle girth had been deliberately cut."

"This is simply incredible," George whispered. "Why did you not say anything before?"

Althea felt him stiffen beside her. Men and their stupid pride, she thought. His feelings were wounded because she had not confided in him. She swallowed her exasperation and apologized sweetly. "George, it was not my decision. Keswick did not wish *anyone* to know, but I am asking you for your help now."

"I still don't see why you should be so worried. Keswick can look after himself, and what could happen to him in Penrith?"

"The stable lad who cut the saddle girth disappeared the same day," she explained with less than her usual patience. "Keswick has learned that he means to be in Penrith tomorrow and intends to confront the boy. Now do you understand why I do not want him to go alone?"

"No, I do not. Keswick will do far better alone. You must trust his judgment, Althea. Even if you were successful in following him, don't you realize that your presence would put him in even more peril? He would be too busy worrying over your safety to have a care for his own. Althea, my dear, be reasonable."

She turned away from him, not caring how sensible he sounded. She knew in her heart that Keswick was in danger, and if George refused to help her, then she would go after Keswick alone.

Chapter 12

Althea arose unusually early the next day, her mind on Keswick. She had given the matter a great deal of thought. She knew she would need a horse to follow Keswick, and there was only one way she could manage to get her mare out of the stable without arousing suspicion.

She hurried down the hall to Meredith's room. Fortunately, the child was already up and Miss Appletree was laying out her dress.

"I hate to disrupt your schedule," Althea said with a disarming smile, "but I should like to take Meredith riding with me this morning, if you do not object."

"Certainly, Miss Underwood, if that is what you wish," the governess answered with unruffled calm.

"It is only that I promised Mrs. Braithwrite I would look in on her today and she particularly wished to see Meredith," Althea elaborated, knowing the explanation was unnecessary but too nervous to behave more rationally.

Meredith, delighted to be let off from lessons, besieged Althea with questions. "When are we going? Is Papa coming, too? Can we see the baby goat?"

"Lady Meredith, please make an effort to conduct yourself properly. Miss Underwood will undoubtedly reconsider her invitation if you do not stop bouncing about like a hoyden."

Meredith stood still at once, but a glance at Althea was enough to reassure her and she dimpled irrepressibly.

"We shall go as soon as you are ready and have breakfast when we return," Althea said. It was important they leave the house before Keswick. "Send her along when she is ready," she added to Miss Appletree before hurrying back to her own room to dress.

Althea was not kept waiting. She'd barely finished buttoning her habit when Meredith knocked on the door. Hoping to avoid Mary and further explanations, Althea grabbed her hat. Making a game of it, she rushed the child down the stairs and out of the house.

She allowed Meredith to run ahead to the stables, following as rapidly as decorum permitted. She greeted Mason with a semblance of composure, if a trifle out of breath, and calmly requested her mare and Meredith's pony be saddled. She restrained herself from urging the man to hurry but peered nervously over her shoulder every other moment, afraid to see Keswick looming behind her.

Mason returned at last with her mare and Jeremy followed him out with Meredith's pony. As she expected, Althea spotted young Johns just inside the barn saddling a horse. She spoke to Mason, giving a credible imitation of unconcern. "Tell the groom he may as well ride with us."

Mason grinned. "It's his lordship's orders, Miss Underwood. I hope you understand."

"Quite all right, Mason. Just ask him to hurry. I promised Mrs. Braithwrite we would call early this morning."

Althea did not breathe easily until they were well clear of the house. There was still no sign of Keswick and she relaxed a little in the saddle. Young Johns's attention, fortunately, was on Meredith, who chattered away as though there was not a thing wrong in the world on this beautiful, sunny morning.

She waited impatiently until they had covered two miles and then enacted a scene for the groom's benefit. "Oh, drat. Johns, I have forgotten the tonic I promised Mrs. Braithwrite, and it is the reason for our visit this morning. You go ahead with Lady Meredith. I shall just ride back to the house, collect it, and then catch up with you."

"But, Miss Underwood—"

"Do not worry, Johns. Just keep a careful eye on Lady Meredith and tell Mrs. Braithwrite I shall be along directly." Not giving the groom a chance to argue, she turned her mare and booted her into a gallop.

She judged she would have an hour or two at best before it occurred to the groom to bring Lady Meredith back with him and search for her. He would be concerned when he couldn't find her, but Althea promised herself that she would make it up to him later.

She prayed she was right in guessing that Keswick would wish an early start. Only one road led to Penrith. Keswick would have to ride east and Althea veered in that direction, heading directly for a small wooded area near the road. From there she would have a restricted view of anyone passing.

215

She dismounted, led the mare in beneath the trees, and patted her reassuringly. She could barely see the road, which she found comforting, for it also meant she could not be seen.

Her stomach growled, reminding her she had not eaten breakfast. She shifted her position, trying not to think of such mundane things as buttered scones and hot chocolate. Surely Keswick should have been along by now, she thought impatiently. Unless she had somehow missed him. Or had he changed his mind? Perhaps he had become suspicious when he learned she'd ridden out early with Meredith.

Doubts assailed her and she was nearly ready to abandon her scheme when she heard the distinctive sound of a carriage. She cautioned the mare to be quiet and, with a hand over the animal's nose, peered through the branches. It was Keswick, driving his yellow curricle with a team of matched bays. Her heart accelerated as he passed, but he never glanced in her direction. He was too intent on handling his high-spirited horses.

Althea allowed him a few minutes, carefully counting off the seconds, before she dared to lead her mare out. She could barely see him in the distance and she didn't believe he would think to look behind him. Nevertheless, she waited until he rounded the bend in the road before setting off after him. She put her mare to a brisk trot. The weather was perfect. Under other circumstances Althea would have enjoyed the ride, but now her mind was preoccupied with Keswick and his meeting with the stable lad.

Grimsby was small, hardly more than a boy.

Keswick easily outweighed him and would have little trouble overcoming him in a one-on-one confrontation. *If* he had the opportunity. Keswick seemed to think he had nothing to fear from Grimsby. He didn't intend to prosecute and only wanted information from the boy. But Grimsby would not know that, and Althea feared he would react like a cornered rat. She doubted he would give Keswick a chance to explain anything.

She wondered if Grimsby was armed. He must know he could be brought up on charges of attempted murder, and an earl's word would carry a great deal of weight. Her lively imagination drew a horrifying picture of Keswick hailing Grimsby as he strolled down the street. The boy would turn, see Nemesis closing in on him, and shoot. Keswick would never have a chance. She spurred her mare, but the going was slow now, with the road winding up the side of the mountain.

She played the scenario in her head over and over, struggling to find a solution. There must be something she could do. Even if it was only to provide a diversion. The mare faltered and Althea leaned forward, encouraging her. The road was a much-traveled one but not very well maintained. In the winter it became totally impassable if there were heavy snowfalls. In the summer the dust became unbearable, as it was now. Althea longed for something cool to drink. Her mare, too, was panting slightly and Althea eased the pace.

Rounding a bend, she could see several miles ahead, but there was no sign of Keswick. Could he already be on the downward descent? She strained her eyes for a glimpse of the yellow curricle, but nothing moved ahead of her. It took another twenty minutes to reach the top of the mountain and at last the road began to gradually curve down. The view was spectacular, the valley below looking like a miniature village, but Althea could not admire it. Keswick was nowhere in sight, and the sheer drop from the side of the road made her dizzy. She nudged her horse closer to the massive stone walls forming the inner core of the mountain.

On the next turn she glanced down and finally spotted him. The sun was well up, glinting brightly off the yellow curricle. Keswick raced along as though he were on a straightaway instead of a perilous, twisting mountain road. She knew he could drive to an inch, but she thought it insane to run such risks on this road. "Stupid man," she muttered aloud, spurring her own mare as he disappeared around a hairpin turn.

She glimpsed him again on the next bend and suddenly felt foolish for chasing after him. He was supremely confident of his abilities and would probably laugh at her fears. The idea she'd conceived in the dark of night, when everything loomed more terrifying, now seemed ludicrous. The sun beating warmly against her back made her drowsy. It seemed impossible for trouble to be lurking on such a peaceful, lazy morning.

She was on the verge of turning back when a shot rang out.

The explosion shattered the stillness of the morning. Althea saw Keswick fall back into the carriage and his horses rear. Terror engulfed her. Had he been shot? Was he wounded? Her own mare tried to bolt and she struggled to bring the animal under control. She was barely aware of what she was doing, her attention still focused on the shiny yellow curricle.

Althea feared Keswick's high-spirited bays would bolt and there was no way she could reach them in time to prevent it. Then she saw a rider approaching from the other direction. Like a harbinger of death, he was clad entirely in black and astride a black stallion. Filmore. Her mind registered the thought numbly, a wave of horror washing over her. She screamed even as she used her crop to urge the mare forward. It was useless. She was too far away.

The tableau disappeared from her view as she raced around the last bend, but it was frozen in her heart. Her eyes strained for a glimpse of the carriage as she cleared the grade above them. She saw Filmore at once. He'd dismounted and was at the front of the curricle near the horses. She wondered fleetingly what he was about before realizing that he had drawn the carriage to the edge of the cliff. She watched him unharness the bays.

She screamed soundlessly, her cries locked in her throat. He meant to plunge the carriage over the cliff—with Keswick in it.

Filmore whirled about suddenly. Althea saw Keswick sitting up in the carriage. *He was alive.* There was no time to be thankful. The figure in black was struggling to climb aboard the curricle.

Althea pulled her mare up and watched in horrified fascination. The two men were locked in a deadly embrace. There was nothing she could do but pray. The two figures seemed of equal size, but she feared Keswick was wounded. She saw him reel when Filmore hit him in the stomach and her heart stopped beating. Then Filmore staggered

219

back. The carriage lurched precariously, one wheel dangling over the edge of the cliff. Keswick jumped for the road and the sudden shift in weight sent it plunging over the side. A bloodcurdling scream filled the air. Althea closed her eyes, near to fainting.

It had all occurred in a matter of moments, but the terror of those last few seconds would stay with her forever. She opened her eyes and saw Keswick on his knees in the road. As he struggled to his feet, she urged the mare forward, anxiously calling his name.

He looked up to see her riding toward him and stared in disbelief. Althea reined in her mare beside him, wordlessly sliding from the saddle into his waiting arms. He crushed her to him in a viselike grip. She reveled in the solid feel of his body against hers and in the strength of the arms that enfolded her. She felt his heart beating rapidly as he pressed her close, heard his heavy, ragged breathing. It was the most comforting sound she'd ever heard.

Keswick loosened his embrace and drew back just enough to gaze down at her. She tilted her head, returning his look in a timeless gesture of surrender. Then her eyes closed as his lips possessed hers with a near savage passion, which she returned in full measure. The kiss was a celebration of life, tasting all the sweeter after his narrow brush with death.

It was to be expected, once the initial shock had passed, that he would scold her for daring to follow him. He did so, but with such frequent pauses to taste her lips, to feel the enticing curves of her body, that his words had little effect. Eventually, however, the reality of the world settled about them. He left her for a few moments to tie up the horses and Althea edged near the side of the road, staring down at the sheer drop.

Jagged rocks and outcroppings of brush covered the side of the mountain. She was too high up to see Filmore, or what might be left of his body. All she could see were flashes of yellow here and there, where pieces of the shattered curricle had flown apart. Nausea swirled in her stomach, surging up into her throat.

Keswick pulled her back from the edge.

Althea hid her face against his shoulder, crying helplessly. She felt his hands caressing her back and took comfort from the soothing murmur of his words. She finally lifted her head. "I never thought Filmore—"

"It was not Jack," he interrupted, then added gently, "I am sorry, Thea. I thought you knew it was George."

"George?" she repeated stupidly, unable to comprehend what he was saying.

"Dressed to look like Filmore in case anyone chanced to see him." He felt her trembling and tightened his arms about her.

"But your own cousin . . . how could he? I cannot believe him capable of such a thing," she said, and escaping from his arms, she walked a few feet away. "He accused me once of wanting you because you had the title and the estate, but I thought he was just distraught . . . just talking, you know, because I had . . ."

"Refused to marry him?" he asked softly when

she paused. He stepped behind her and enclosed her in his arms again.

She nodded, blushing as she recalled the scene in the drawing room when George had proposed.

Keswick turned her to face him and tenderly brushed her hair back from her brow. "Do not blame yourself, Thea. There was nothing you could have said or done to change the order of things. It started long before you ever came to Cumberland."

"You suspected him then?"

"Not until recently. I knew he had always been envious of me, but I couldn't believe he hated me enough to go to these lengths."

She shuddered and reached up a hand to caress his face. "Keswick, I told him you were driving to Penrith today. I wanted his help—"

"So that is how he knew. I wondered. I was not expecting any trouble this morning, not until he took a shot at me."

"I thought you were hit," she said, her eyes reflecting the horror she'd felt earlier.

"No, the bullet grazed the seat. It was a near thing though, and I thought it better to let him think I was wounded, but I had no idea you were watching." He bent his head and kissed her again, tenderly this time, until at last her body stopped trembling and some of the fear left her eyes.

When they arrived in the stable yard, chaos reigned. Mason ran from the stables with young Johns close behind him, while a dozen other men crowded about them.

"We was just setting up a search party to go

looking for you, Miss Underwood. Young Johns here was certain something awful had happened to you."

She cringed at the look of concern on the groom's face as he helped her down. She had totally forgotten him, and he must have been frantic. She gave him her hand. "Please forgive me for worrying you so, Johns. I never meant—" She broke off, tears filling her eyes.

"Aw, it don't matter none so long as you're all right," he assured her, head down. "I brought Lady Meredith back. She's inside with Miss Appletree."

Althea squeezed his hand gratefully before turning to the house. She missed the look of total devotion on the lad's face. Keswick saw it, however, and smiled to himself. Althea seemed to have that effect on many people.

Cheever met them at the door and so far forgot himself as to express his relief at seeing Miss Underwood safely home. "The sight of you will do Miss Carlyle a world of good, miss. She's in the blue drawing room."

Althea thanked him in her soft voice and, with a mute appeal to Keswick, started down the hall. Telling Aunt Pysie about George would be the worst of this affair. She opened the door of the drawing room and paused. A young gentleman, his back to them, was comforting Aunt Pysie in his arms. He swung around at the sound of the door and Althea stared at him in considerable surprise.

Lord Filmore looked years younger in a finely tailored coat of light blue. So much so that it took Althea a few seconds to recognize him. They both started to speak at once, then broke off as Aunt Pysie let out a cry of delight.

"Althea, oh, child, I have been so dreadfully worried. Where on earth have you been? Are you all right?" She barely gave her a chance to answer. She waddled across the room and embraced Althea warmly, while the two men looked at each other awkwardly.

Filmore smiled hesitantly and then stepped forward, extending his hand. "I do not believe I have had the chance to properly welcome you home, Andrew."

Keswick took his hand, gripping it in a firm clasp. "It's good to see you here, Jack."

Aunt Pysie released Althea, although she kept hold of her hand and drew her toward the sofa. "Jack has been such a comfort. When they told me you had disappeared, Thea, I did not know what to do. And then he came and he organized the men into a search party and—oh, dear heavens, someone must let them know you are back."

"They know, Aunt Pysie," Althea reassured her. "I am sorry to have given you such a fright. It has been a . . . a horrendous morning."

"What is it? What has happened?" Aunt Pysie asked fearfully as she read the distress in Althea's eyes. She turned to Keswick. "Is it George?"

Althea gasped. "How did you know?"

Aunt Pysie did not answer. Her eyes were focused on Keswick and she waited for his answer. The only sign of alarm she gave was the way her hand continued to grip Althea's tightly.

Keswick told her haltingly of what had passed. Aunt Pysie, for once, listened without interruption.

She did not cry or faint, as Althea expected, but the color drained from her face.

"It is what I feared, although I prayed it was not so," Aunt Pysie said, her voice heavy with sorrow. "I am only thankful his mother is not alive to bear the burden of this. It would have crushed her. I think I should like to be alone now, if you will excuse me." She rose shakily to her feet and Althea stood with her.

"No, child, you stay here with Andrew and Jack. I shall be better directly, but I need a few moments to myself."

Althea watched her leave and then turned to Keswick. "I can hardly believe she suspected it was George, but she was not in the least surprised."

He shook his head. "She knew. Remember when she was talking about the lump of clay? I looked it up later, just out of curiosity. The verse goes: 'Hath not the potter power over the clay, of the same lump to make one vessel unto honour, and another unto dishonour?' "

"And you and George were from the same lump," Filmore said, hastily adding, "So to speak. She is a shrewd old girl in her own way. I thought I was the only one who fancied George might be willing to do away with you."

"Not you, too," Althea said, collapsing into a wing chair. "Why did no one think to warn me?"

Filmore grinned disarmingly. She realized again how much younger he looked. The gray eyes had lost their hardness and the grim lines about his mouth nearly disappeared when he smiled.

"I could not say much, not when you half suspected I was the culprit. I doubt you would have believed me."

"I never—" she started to protest.

"It was quite understandable, really, given the way I was behaving." He turned to look at Keswick. "Can you forgive me, Andrew? I have been a fool wasting all these years."

"If you can forgive me," Keswick replied grimly. "Both of you. If I had not been such a coward, running off to Europe as I did, we might have resolved a lot of problems long ago—and George might not be lying at the bottom of a mountain."

"Keswick, you must not blame yourself," Althea cried, unable to bear the haunted look in his eyes. "If anyone is to be held responsible for George's death, it must be me. I allowed him to believe that there might be a chance for us . . . even when I knew in my heart that I could never marry him. Perhaps, if I had not encouraged him . . ."

Filmore stood up abruptly. "I suggest the pair of you talk to Aunt Pysie. No doubt she will come up with an appropriate scripture. Something like 'Death borders upon our birth, and our cradle stands in the grave.' Do not look so surprised, Andrew. Your aunt is not the only one who can quote the Bible. I have had ample time to ponder those words and come to the conclusion that our destiny is written in the stars. There is little point in fighting against it."

"Do you honestly believe our lives are preordained?" Keswick asked as he stood to shake hands with his old friend.

"Who can say for certain?" Jack shrugged. "But I would not advise struggling against something so obviously meant to be." He paused, glancing at

Althea and then back at Keswick. "I shall leave you two to sort it out, but I hope you mean to invite me to the wedding. I might even be available to act as groomsman, should you have need of me."

Keswick grinned broadly, but Althea blushed and would not look at him.

Filmore halted, his hand on the door. "Speaking of weddings, the reason I rode over was to tell you the latest news. The village is buzzing. Seems Miss Regina Montague ran off last night. She left a note for her aunt that she was eloping to Gretna Green. With Richard Kingsly."

The door closed behind him and Althea immediately became busy gathering the cups from the tea table. "Poor Mrs. Harding. She must be terribly upset with Regina. And to run off with Kingsly of all people—"

"Althea," Keswick said softly, his voice disturbingly near.

She wiped at an imaginary spot on the table. "I quite thought she considered the locals beneath her—"

"Althea, leave that be. Mrs. Pennington will take care of it. And forget about Miss Montague. There is something I wish to say to you and I should like to have your undivided attention."

Her hand stilled even as her pulse raced. She wondered if he could hear how loudly her heart was beating. She sat back, folding her hands tightly together, and then dared to look up at his dearly beloved face.

He reached down for her hand, intending to pull her to her feet, when someone tapped on the door. She clearly heard the curse that escaped his lips and echoed the sentiment. Miss Appletree opened the door.

"I am sorry to intrude, my lord, but Lady Meredith will not settle down until she has seen for herself that Miss Underwood is quite safe. I fear she overheard some nonsense from the maids that Miss Underwood had disappeared."

Meredith darted around the governess and scampered across the room to Althea, catapulting into her arms. Althea laughingly caught her and held her tightly for a moment. Then she felt the wetness of tears against her neck.

"Meredith? What is it, darling? I am perfectly safe as you can see. Hush now, there is no reason for you to cry."

"I thought you left me," the little girl sobbed, her words muffled.

"As though I would! Whatever gave you such a notion?"

"I heard Mary say you might have to go away because of Papa," Meredith said, lifting her head to look at her. She saw Althea glance helplessly at Keswick and turned her own eyes to him. "Papa, don't make her go away. I love Aunt Thea best in the whole world."

Keswick knelt beside the chair and reached a hand out to caress his daughter's hair. "I love her, too, princess, and I promise you that if I have anything to say in the matter, Althea will never leave this house. But I need to talk to her about it. Will you go upstairs with Miss Appletree while I try to convince Thea to stay with us?"

Meredith nodded solemnly. Keswick wiped away a tear on her cheek with the tip of his finger before lifting her down. He handed her over to Miss Appletree with a smile.

"I shall be up to see you in a few moments, Meredith," Althea called from her chair as the child looked hesitantly back at her.

Keswick shut the door firmly behind him. He stood leaning against it, his dark eyes intent on Althea. "I wonder if it is possible in this house to achieve five minutes alone with you."

"I should not think it likely we would be interrupted now, my lord," she said demurely. She stood, her brown eyes glowing.

It was an invitation he was incapable of resisting and seconds later he held her firmly in his arms. His lips found hers and he forgot the words he meant to say. Forgot everything as she returned his kisses, her slim body pressing against his.

When he raised his head, he heard her muted whisper of protest. The sound filled him with unbearable joy. He gazed down at her in wonder that so small a frame, just a slip of a girl, could turn his world upside down.

Althea opened her eyes and saw the emotion in his. It was the same look he had given her in the ballroom, the look of love she'd thought she'd only imagined. His gaze combined tenderness and passion, and it shook her to the tips of her toes. His hand came up to trace the line of her lips and she kissed his fingertips.

Keswick drew in a ragged breath at that simple gesture of her devotion. "Althea, dearest . . . say you will marry me. I have waited so long for you."

"Have you, sir? And with single-minded devotion, I suppose?" she asked with a smile, contentedly resting in his arms. Assured of his love, she could tease him now. And she did not intend to let him off so easily. "What of Lizzie and Miss Montague and that elegant creature from Paris? Do you deny they attracted your attention?"

His teeth gleamed in a devilish smile. "I am glad to see that at least something I planned worked. Were you a little jealous, Thea? Just a tiny bit? I hoped that if you saw that other women found me attractive, you might reconsider how you felt about me."

The catch in his voice when he said the last words was her undoing. She flung her arms about him and murmured into his neck, "Oh, Keswick, how could you be such a fool?"

"May I take that to mean you will marry me?" he asked, his mouth warm against her ear.

"Yes, oh, yes. . . ."

It is doubtful they heard the noise at the door. Certainly they did not see it open slightly or hear Miss Appletree's whispered admonishment. Meredith's voice, however, with its high, sweet tones, clearly floated in to them.

"Why is Papa kissing Aunt Thea?"

He drew back slightly, smiling down at the woman in his arms, and then raised his voice enough to carry into the hall. "Papa is going to marry Aunt Thea. Now close the door and go away."

The door shut decidedly as Meredith let out a most unladylike and exuberant yell. Miss Appletree and Cheever were too pleased to chastise her and exchanged a knowing glance. Aunt Pysie, coming down the stairs, regained some of her color, and was heard to remark that she believed Eugenia Yardley had a very good fertility potion. Just the thing for a young bride.